the CONQUEST

THE CONQUEST SERIES BOOK ONE

MARY FRANCIS

Second edition, February 2018
Published by Curiosity Press

© Copyright 2018 Mary Francis

ISBN: 978-1-912775-05-7

HISTORICAL NOTES

ANGLO-SAXON SOCIETY

Since the days of King Alfred the Great, education was encouraged for girls as well as boys. Alfred himself was a very learned man who valued education.

Women in Anglo Saxon society had almost equal status as men, could own property in their own right and ruled their households. In religious life it was not unknown for women to be Abbesses and in charge of the whole community of monks as well as nuns.

When couples married, the future husband was required to give a gift of money to his wife to provide for her in case she was later divorced or widowed. Marriages were usually arranged, often when children were very young, at least among wealthier families – it was important to align with families of like standing. Peasants were more likely to marry where they wished.

Life was ruled by the seasons, people living in small communities and raising their own food and producing most of their own clothing. The food was not much different from today, such as meat, vegetables, fruits, grains, fish, milk and cheese, and honey for sweetening. Broth – a thick soup – stews, gruel – made with grains and similar to porridge – and meat roasted on a spit, similar to our rotisserie, would all be familiar today. Such things as sugar and spices were available only to the very rich as they had to be imported. Tea, coffee, chocolate, potatoes, pineapples, bananas and other exotic foods had not yet been introduced.

Homes were very primitive by today's standards, especially for the poorer classes. Wattle and daub walls and thatch roofed homes, often only one room where all the family lived together. The floor mostly just earth, hardened by years of sweeping and being walked on, with a fire pit in the centre of the room. There was no chimney, the smoke from the fire allowed to drift through the thatch where it kept most of the insects and small creatures at bay, the earliest form of pest control.

These people may have been poor by today's standards, but they were free and often owned their own land.

The coming of the Normans changed all that, turning most into serfs who owned nothing. Women were no longer considered of any importance, they belonged to men, their father or husband. In fact it was not until the twentieth century that women regained the rights that Anglo Saxon women took for granted.

THE NORMANS

For centuries the Vikings (pirates) from Scandinavia – a race of intrepid seamen and ferocious fighters, who had travelled as far away from their homeland as the Mediterranean and even to the coast of North America, where they established a settlement - had been harassing the eastern coast of England and northern coast of France. In the year nine hundred and eleven, King Charles (the simple) of France ceded a large section of his country to Rollo, the leader of a band of Vikings, on the understanding that they would leave the rest of France alone, and also protect the northern coast from other invaders. Rollo became known as Duke Rollo and the area they lived in as Normandy – land of the Norsemen.

William, Duke of Normandy was a descendant of Duke Rollo, the illegitimate son of Duke Robert. He was known as the Bastard by his enemies, including many of his own countrymen who did not agree with him being heir to the Dukedom. He was related, by marriage, to the royal house of England, and cousin to Harold Godwinson.

Later propaganda by the Normans insisted that the throne of England was promised to William by Edward the Confessor and confirmed by Harold with a vow on holy relics, when he visited the court of Normandy several years earlier.

The Vikings intermarried with the local population and adopted their language, manners and customs, but they were still Norsemen, Vikings with a French veneer.

WAR

War is ugly and brutal. It is true today and was even more so in Medieval times. Especially it was true as a conquering army ravished the country they had invaded. William of Normandy was no exception. As his troops invaded England they butchered, raped and pillaged their way through the country, dispossessing the Saxon people and inflicting severe punishment on any who disobeyed the harsh laws that were introduced. William rewarded his Norman friends and those who had supported his claim to the English throne by giving them large tracts of land as long as they continued to support him by supplying him with armies whenever he needed to keep the Saxons in good order. High born Saxons or lowly peasants were treated without compassion or concern for their plight. Homeless people wandered the land often descending into outlawry to sustain themselves.

This is the background to the story "The Conquest." It is not sugar coated, sanitised or presented in any way to make it pleasant reading for modern day readers. Rather I have tried to write it as realistically as possible as a testament to the courage, bravery and determination of the survivors. Rothwynn is one of those resolved to overcome this new and hostile world by making a loving marriage and a good and happy life for herself and her family.

x

GLOSSARY

Wattle and Daub: A composite building material used for making walls. A woven lattice of wood strips – the wattle – is daubed with a sticky substance made with some combination of wet soil, clay, sand, animal dung and straw.

Witan: In Anglo Saxon England, a supreme council of wise men or King's council, usually Earls.

Midden/Privy: Some kind of trash heap. Also a very primitive toilet. Often a cess pit or dung heap. When it was used as a toilet it was usually in a small building to give a bit of shelter and privacy, and called a privy. Used by the whole household.

Lyre: A stringed instrument with five to seven strings. Mostly oval shaped and held in a similar position to a hand held harp. Often used to accompany poems and stories such as Beowulf.

Beowulf: The oldest surviving epic poem of Old English written by an anonymous Anglo Saxon poet sometime between the eighth and tenth century.

Fief: Inherited or rights granted by an overlord to a vassal who held it in return for a form of allegiance and service.

Demesne: All the land which was retained by the Lord of the Manor for his own use and support and under his own management.

Mead: An alcoholic beverage made with honey and water, often with the addition of fruits, spices, grains or hops. Very popular with the Saxons.

Morning Gift: A gift of money given by the groom to the bride the morning after the marriage had taken place. This was hers to use as she wished. It was to ensure that both she and her children were provided for if she became widowed or if she and her husband separated. Divorce was granted only for adultery, but they could separate. Then property and money was divided equally between them.

The Hall: The Hall or Great Hall, was used by all the household. It was where all the servants, tenants and employees would eat and often where some of them also slept. It provided no privacy for anyone.

Cotswold: Comes from the word "cot" meaning a pen or shelter for sheep, and "wold" meaning rolling hills. An area stretching from northern Wiltshire, through the county of Gloucestershire and the west of Oxfordshire to the southern part of Warwickshire. Typically the houses in this area are built of the local honey coloured limestone, giving the villages a unique look.

ABOUT THE AUTHOR

For all of my adult life English history has been my passion. It began when I was a teenager and read all my mother's Georgette Heyer novels. From there I became engrossed in Jane Austen, the Brontes and Jean Plaidy, gradually defining my interest in and love for medieval history. My circle of authors widened to include Ellis Peters, Phillipa Gregory and many others. I not only read fiction but studied historians such as Alison Weir, Simon Schama, David Starkey and Winston Churchill's History of the English Speaking People.

Living in England has given me the opportunity to visit places where world changing events took place. Pre-historical Stonehenge, Battle Abbey, the Tower of London, and Runneymede, where Magna Carta was signed, to name just a few.

From the time of my first visit to the Cotswolds and Castle Combe, where I fell in love with the beauty of the place, I began to wonder what it would have been like to live in medieval times when the area became rich from the wool trade, and how major events would have impacted the people who lived there. Slowly the idea of the Conquest series formed in my mind - a fictional Saxon settlement, not far from Castle Combe.

This then, is the beginning...

PROLOGUE

It was the first warm and balmy day of the year and as Aerlene sat on the bench in the little wooden chapel, listening to the priest telling more stories from the Bible, she realised it was most certainly not a day to be inside the stuffy building having lessons. It was a day to be running on the beach enjoying the breeze ruffling her hair as it wafted over the sea and across the sand.

She could hardly wait until Father Eldred dismissed them and she would be free for the remainder of the day…free to run home for a bowl of broth and then down the cliffs to the water's edge, and at least for a short while, have nothing to do but enjoy herself.

It was the year of our Lord one thousand and twenty one. Aerlene and her family lived in Wessex, less than a mile from the south coast of England. She loved the sea and the beach. She loved the feel of it all; the chill of the water on her feet, the salt spray on her face, the freedom she felt as she gathered shells, hunted through the rock pools for small crabs, or popped the seaweed between her fingers, at one with the sea and the sky.

At last she was there, lessons over, chores done and free to spend some time in the sun. She didn't have very long before she would have to return home and take care of the young ones while her mother supervised the servants in the preparation of the evening meal. As soon as the warmth left the sun and it began to lower in the sky she would have to leave, so she would make the most of every minute.

Aerlene was twelve years old, slowly changing from child to young woman, determined to enjoy her youth while it lasted, before she'd be wed to a young man chosen for her by her father, a thought she constantly pushed from her mind. She had no wish to grow up or to marry. Her childhood was precious and full of happiness. Everything seemed right with her world.

Her father was a stern and authoritative figure and somewhat distant, but her mother, her brothers – even if they were a bit bossy - and sisters were all very loving and close. She was going to be a beautiful young woman too, with golden hair, long and lustrous, deep blue eyes that seemed to find the world interesting and amusing, and a smile and giggle that were contagious.

The sea was icy cold on her feet as she wiggled her toes in the sand so instead, she knelt and built a small fort, then found some shells to decorate the tower. With her back to the sea and engrossed in her enjoyment of the day, she didn't see the approach of the ships. Dragon ships. Five of them. A raiding party of Vikings coming most unexpectedly from the west, possibly from Ireland.

It was unusual to see them in this part of the channel. Usually they came from the north and east and didn't venture this far west. No one would be expecting them. Some small sound alerted her and she turned just in time to see the last ship round the point and the first pull to the shore, to see a Viking warrior, looking like the devil himself with fire in his eyes and a knife between his teeth, leap from his boat and run up the beach towards her.

She stood transfixed, frozen with terror. Then, lifting her skirts, Aerlene ran faster than she'd ever run in her life. She was petrified and fear gave wind to her feet. She pounded up the beach towards the path that led to the cliffs...the cliffs she would have to climb to escape the menace that was now beating down upon her.

Closer and ever closer she could hear him coming, feel the drumming of his feet on the shingle behind her. Now sobbing, the stones cutting into her feet, still she ran, faster and faster, praying she wouldn't fall and praying for some miracle to save her from the marauders. She'd heard horrific tales of what they'd do to her if they caught her.

On and on she went until she was within reach of the footpath. With a lunge, the closest raider grabbed at her skirt and dragged her down. She screamed again and again. He just laughed as he threw her to the ground, tied her hands together, bundled her over his shoulder, carried her back down the beach and tossed her into his boat.

It was all over now. Aerlene didn't know what had happened to her village...to her people. They had taken other prisoners; young, strong and healthy as she was, some from her village, others she didn't know. What had happened to her family? Had they escaped? Or were they all dead?

She sat huddled in the back of the boat, shivering with cold and fear. If only she'd been more alert. She could have seen the small fleet coming and warned the villagers of the danger, giving them time to escape, to hide in the forest. But instead, she'd been intent on enjoying the day, thinking only of her own pleasure. As long as she lived she would never forgive herself.

Normandy, and the busy market place in the small town was filled with slaves for sale; pretty blonde girls and strong young men. The bidders were eager and the raiders made good money for their merchandise. Aerlene was bought, along with another girl and three young men, by one Gilbert De Sellé, and taken to the castle that would become her home for the rest of her life. They were the lucky ones as Gilbert was a just and fair man.

Aerlene became a servant to his wife who treated her kindly. She was his second wife - his first had died in childbirth. His son, too, had not lived. Aerlene's new mistress was now with child and spent hours praying for the safe delivery of a son. Aerlene soon realised that these Normans were very devout. Saxons were Christian too, but they were much more relaxed in their devotions. Alas, these prayers went unanswered. When the time finally came for the child to be delivered, neither mother nor child survived.

Gilbert was almost inconsolable, not so much that he grieved for his wife as he'd never really loved her. It was an arranged marriage and he could easily find another wife, but the death of this second baby son was hard to be borne. He hid himself away for weeks on end, eating barely enough to stay alive. Eventually he emerged from his grief and took up the reins of running his estate once again.

The weeks turned into months and the months into years. By now Aerlene was sixteen years old and the promise of her beauty had been fulfilled. One day she realised that Gilbert was watching her, looking at her differently, making her uncomfortable and embarrassed, so she tried to avoid him, making sure that when he was around she was busy in some other part of the castle, until one day he came into the dairy where she'd gone to get some supplies for the kitchen. She turned to leave.

"No!" he commanded her curtly. "Don't go. I wish to talk to you."

She stopped and curtsied to him, keeping her head bowed so he could not see her face.

He tilted her head up with his hand beneath her chin and looked at her long and hard; her face, her body, as though he could see her naked. She could feel herself hot with shame, her skin burning as he touched her.

"You have been happy here?" he asked, his voice now kind and gentle.

"Everyone has been very good to me, my lord," she responded softly, her head bowed again in submission to his will, forcing herself to remain motionless.

Still he looked at her, studying her for several minutes, then turned and walked swiftly from the building and as he left she heard him say to himself, "Yes, yes. She'll do very well."

Later that same day the housekeeper approached her. "Girl, you are to bathe and dress in clean clothes then go to the master's chamber."

"Oh no, please no," she begged in no more than a whisper.

"You will do as you are told. I do not have to remind you that you are a slave here. He owns you, body and soul. You have an hour then he expects you. You will go with a smile on your face and happily and freely give yourself to him," the woman's voice angry and determined.

"I cannot," Aerlene sobbed.

"Unless you want to be whipped, you most certainly will," was the harsh response she received.

This was almost worse than the day when the Vikings came and stole her away from her home in England. At least then she had some small hope that they might not catch her, or that she might escape. Now there was none.

All hope was gone as she realised what her future held. Aerlene knew she would never get away and she understood what he would be demanding from her.

Less than an hour later she was standing outside his door, wearing the new clothes that had been provided, her hair still damp from her bath and softly curling around her face. She was trembling from head to toe, the housekeeper holding her firmly by her side. The older woman knocked at the door and entered as they heard his voice, "Come."

"Here she is my lord," she said pulling Aerlene roughly behind her. "I hope you will be pleased with her. She is a good girl and has had nothing to do with men before, as I told you."

"Thank you Agnetta. That will be all now. I do not want to be disturbed. Not, I think, for a long time."

Once more he stood and stared at her. Aerlene bit her lip trying not to cry or to show her fear.

"You understand why you are here?" he wanted to know.

A small nod was all she could manage.

"Aerlene, isn't it?"

Another nod.

"Well, Aerlene, we are going to know each other very well before this day is out. I have waited a long time for this." And he walked towards her, his hands outstretched eagerly reaching for her while the tears ran unchecked down her cheeks.

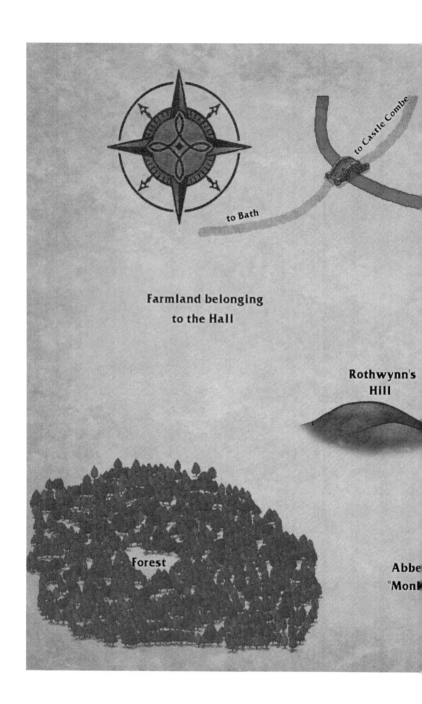

THE CONQUEST
IITH CENTURY

Abbey
farmland

Saxon Hall

Abbey
Cloisters

Compound

s

Church

Abbey
farmland

bey farmland
nk's Meadow"

CHAPTER 1

*R*obert stood on the shore staring out to sea, a look of complete concentration on his face. In his mind's eye he could see the distant land; the waves crashing onto the beach, the cliff face towering above, even hear the call of the gulls as they swooped in the clean, fresh air. England.

He'd heard about England all his life as his mother had told him much of her childhood there; how she'd loved the beach and the sea; how she'd spent so much time playing in the coastal countryside near her home with her brothers, sisters and cousins, and he'd longed to see her homeland.

Now the opportunity was coming - his waiting and yearning almost over. Soon, soon please God, they would go.

They'd been waiting for weeks now. Waiting for the wind to change direction, enabling them to cross the channel. Duke William had mustered his army early in August. They'd gathered at the mouth of the river Somme, on the northern coast of France, a massive invasion force, more than seven hundred ships that were partially loaded with supplies, and almost eight thousand men camped on the shore with horses and armaments for them all.

But the waiting time was wearing Robert down. He worked his men hard, making sure their fitness was at it's peak, keeping their confidence strong and their enthusiasm high.

Robert himself was not happy at the prospect of invading his mother's country. If it wasn't for his father's dying wish, and his own belief that the cause was just, he would have refused to go. But an oath had been broken. The Pope had given his approval and wrongs must be righted. So he was here halfway through September and still watching the sea and waiting for the wind to turn in their favour.

As he stood his mind wandered back to his childhood, back to the days when he sat at his mother's knee and listened in awe to the stories she told of her Saxon village in Wessex, of her father, the chief of their village, and his bravery in defending his people from invading Vikings.

They came rarely in those days and maybe her father had exaggerated his prowess, but she'd enjoyed the stories he told, of heroic days long since passed and the daring deeds of her ancestors.

The great king Alfred who had burnt the cakes, if the story was to be believed, then defeated the Danes.

And other kings like Athelston, and Edgar, the first to rule all of England, and of the Danish king, Canute, sitting on his chair at Bosham harbour commanding the tide to retreat. Robert had been enthralled as she re-told the tales.

Robert's childhood had been happy, full of love and precious family times. His mother had made it so. He'd adored her and remembered asking his father once why she was so much more beautiful than the other women.

"Your mother is Saxon from England, not a Norman like us. The Saxon women have fair skin, blue eyes and golden hair, and yes, she is very beautiful. We are lucky to have her. I thank the good Lord every day for bringing her into my life."

And so he asked his mother more questions about her life before she came to Normandy and why and how she came. He learned about the Viking raid and how she was sold as a slave and how fortunate she felt that it was his father who had bought her and how kind he had been to her. And then he had married her and they'd been a happy family ever since.

He wanted to know what it was like to be a slave and how had it happened that his father had wanted to marry her, so she told him about that too. How she hadn't known Gilbert much at first, she'd still been a child, but as she matured he'd noticed her and taken her to his bed. She'd been frightened of him but he was gentle and kind and loved her dearly and then they'd married and he'd treated her so well she'd learned to love him too.

Although she always missed her homeland, she didn't regret what had happened with her and Gilbert and was forever grateful for her wonderful family. Then she had smiled at Robert and ruffled his hair. "If I hadn't come, I wouldn't have you and that would have made me very sad."

Robert was the second child born to Gilbert and Aerlene de Sellé. His brother, another Gilbert, was two years older. He had two sisters, Aline and Adele and the youngest of the family, another boy, Armand. Life was good to the de Sellé family.

They lived in a castle, albeit a rather small one, and Gilbert's family were close associates of the Dukes of Normandy, Gilbert himself being a lifelong friend to William and involved in the political turmoil had by the young heir as he struggled to assert himself over those who would usurp his rights to the Dukedom.

So Robert, as he was growing up, was aware of the situation surrounding his country and aware of the ambition of William and his belief that the crown of England would one day belong to him - certain that it was his right.

Learning to ride his pony almost before he could walk, Robert was trained in military skills while very young. He and his brother Gilbert often had sword fights in their nursery, much to the dismay of their mother and amusement of their younger sisters. Gilbert always won. It infuriated Robert so much that he practiced long hours each day until finally he managed to beat his brother and had to be dragged off him by his mother.

"No, no, no," she had shouted at him. "You shall not kill your brother."

"He won't beat me! He won't ever beat me again," Robert had hissed, his teeth clenched and his face red with fury at his brother, determination to win uppermost in his mind. From that day on, Robert had continued to practice and hone his skills until he was expert in horsemanship and swordplay, defeated by no one.

He was clever too, and very much his mother's favourite, although she tried not to show it. He would spend a lot of time with her, learning her language, listening to the tales of her childhood and asking her questions about her homeland, intrigued at the differences of her experiences from his. There was no doubt that there was a special bond between them. Robert was never ashamed to show his affection for his mother and he'd often openly express his love for her.

It would have worried Gilbert if his son had not also shown such aptitude for fighting. It was a tough world and Robert would have to earn his living as a soldier. The eldest son would inherit his father's castle, title and land. Robert would have to make his own way. Armand, the baby of the family, would be trained for the church, which fortunately for him, was also his natural inclination.

And so life went on for the de Sellé family. As Gilbert was often away with Duke William helping him secure his inheritance, much of the children's education was left to Aerlene to arrange.

Aerlene had come from a distinguished Saxon family with a strong belief in education for girls as well as boys, a tradition handed down from the great King Alfred himself. Her children were all taught to read and write, they were all expected to know Latin, to be knowledgeable in numeracy, and have an understanding of the world around them. Their tutor did not take long to realise that Robert was intelligent and advised his mother to make sure his scholarship was not ignored in preference to his military training.

As the boys grew older, the elder Gilbert often took the younger Gilbert with him as he attended to his duties for Duke William, leaving Robert to take care of things at home. Robert soon became proficient at running the castle and overseeing their farmland. He obviously enjoyed the responsibility his father laid on him and, and when he allowed himself to think about it, was disappointed that he would not be the one to inherit the property.

But as he was usually of a cheerful disposition he didn't worry about it for long, hoping that somehow, someday, somewhere, he would have a place he could call home. It wouldn't have to be a castle or very grand. He just wanted a place where he could establish a dynasty of his own and be as happy and content as his father and mother were.

The good times came to an end when Aerlene died. It was sudden. She had been ill for such a short time. It seemed to Robert that one day she was contentedly running her household and caring for her family and the next day she had gone.

He was inconsolable, spending hours on his own, out on his horse or brooding as he walked through the nearby forest and fields. He didn't ignore the jobs he was assigned to do, his military training or his studies. He even found time to comfort his sisters and young Armand, but all the joy had gone from his life.

Although he would never admit it, and never let anyone see, he often felt his eyes fill with tears and was unable to stop the heartrending sobs that engulfed him. The once happy, cheerful boy had gone forever and was replaced by a grave and sober minded young man, strict in his obedience to religious ritual and knightly observances. He took his duties seriously, pushing himself to greater endurance and ever greater achievement.

As time went on the young Gilbert was married and brought his bride to live at the castle. Before long both their sisters too were wed and gone from home. Young Armand left to join the church as had always been planned. Their father spent more and more time with the Duke, away in various parts of the country. Robert felt he was indeed completely alone.

The day they brought his father home, seriously wounded and close to death, he was at the point when he felt he no longer wanted to live. There seemed to be no point to his life any more. He had no focus and longed for his mother. She'd always been able to comfort and sustain him through difficult times.

Sitting by his father's bedside, thinking he was sleeping, Robert knelt by the bed, put his head in his hands and began praying silently to God, beginning to doubt He would even listen to him. He felt his father's hand, diffidently stroking his hair and glanced up to see his anxious look as he gazed at his son and saw the tears in Robert's eyes.

"You must not fret my boy. I know I'm dying and I'm happy to go. My life has been good and I long to be with your mother now." His voice, already weak, wavered and he struggled to add, "I want you to promise me something."

"Anything, sir. I will do anything that is in my power."

"When I am gone, go to William. He will need all the help he can get from good, loyal followers."

"But, father, it is his plan to invade England. I don't think I can do that – it was mother's home."

"Then you need to be there even more. He needs people who understand the Saxon way of life. It will give you the opportunity to help your mother's people."

Robert was quiet for several minutes as he thought about his father's words. Hesitatingly he answered, "Very well. I will do as you wish."

So he had come. Now he stood on the shore watching the sea…the sea that divided his homeland from his mother's, a tall young man, twenty-seven years old, with dark hair and eyes, of strong build but quite slim, perhaps not handsome but with the kind of face one would not forget. There was something very arresting about him.

In the days when he'd been happy his smile lit up his face and his eyes would twinkle with laughter when something amused him. He had a laugh that was infectious and a sense of fun, but both had been buried for a long time now. There was serious work to be done.

It was time he busied himself and made sure his men did the same. The armour and weaponry must be kept in top condition, ready for the battle that was to come and was the next job on the list. He turned away from the sea and made his way up the beach with a determined step.

It was several more days before the wind finally changed and they were able to embark and sail across the channel towards their fate. They would conquer or die in the attempt. Robert stood on deck watching as they approached the land, the white cliffs looming above the sand getting closer and closer.

They landed at Pevensey. It took hours before they were all on shore with horses, weapons and supplies, but no one hindered them. Had the invading force been seen? Were messages even now being sent across the country to King Harold? Did he know they were here? They went about their business establishing camp, getting things in order.

Within a few days William decided to move further east, to Hastings, and wait…to wait for Harold. They knew the king would soon be there and he had an impressive army. The battle would come. The only question was – when?

Robert waited with them. More than anything he wanted to leave, to head west to find his mother's home…her people. Only because he'd promised his father did he stay, mustered his men and kept them busy, training for the fight that would soon be upon them. He knew they could not afford to relax their guard or to rest. They must be in top condition and ready for anything.

He too, had to be ready. He had to harden his heart towards the English Saxons or he wouldn't be able to fight. He must forget his mother and think only of them as his enemy, enemies that had to be defeated in battle and then subdued by whatever means were necessary.

The fourteenth day of October. King Harold Godwinson and his army had arrived and were arrayed in battle formation at the top of Senlac Hill, William's troops at the bottom. There was no doubt that the Saxons had the advantage, but they'd just come from another battle and a long, forced march from the north. The defending army would not be at their best - they would be tired and weary. The Normans, in the peak of condition, were ready for them. The fateful day was here at last.

CHAPTER 2

To Earl Aedgar, his daughter Rothwynn was his little ray of sunshine. She had the ability to lighten every facet of his life. There was no doubt that he adored her. She was a delightful child, full of fun and laughter. Everyone was happy when she was around.

Now as he sat at the table busy with estate business, he heard her footsteps as she ran towards the door, pulled it open and peeped in at him. Despite himself, he couldn't stop the smile spreading across his face as she entered the room. He held his arms open and she ran to him, circling her arms around his neck. No matter the time of day he always had time for his little daughter.

Rothwynn was quite lovely. Golden hair curled around her face, big, deep blue eyes that always seemed to be amused at life, a tiny dimple in her cheek, a sprinkling of freckles across her nose, and a ready smile for all. Her voice was soft and a little husky and her laughter a joy to all who heard it. She was the youngest, and favourite, of his three children.

The one thing that everyone could agree on about Earl Aedgar, friend or foe alike, was that he was ambitious. If asked, he would say it was for his family's benefit, and he could be quite persuasive in his argument, but those who knew him well never believed him. He'd been ambitious all his life, long before he had a family of his own.

He was a big man. His size alone was somewhat intimidating and his voice booming and deep. He wore his fair hair long, as was the custom among his people, he had a long, bushy beard and piercing blue eyes, the colour of the sea. He was one of the many who mingled with the leading men of the country and was part of the Witan – the group of influential Earls who made all the important decisions of government. Aedgar's land was fertile and rich. His family a tight knit group consisting of his ageing, invalid father, his two grown sons, his daughter and his brother.

As a young man he'd courted and won the hand of a young lady who was a direct descendant of King Alfred through her mother's line. Although she was considered to be quite a beauty, he was not interested in her looks. He wanted her because of her royal connections. In actual fact, he had bought her. Her father was poor and struggled to feed his family – royal blood does not always signify riches – so when Earl Aedgar had offered a magnificent price for the privilege of marrying his daughter, Odelia, it was agreed. What the girl had to say about it was not considered important enough to ask her, but as Aedgar was wealthy and an important and influential earl, it was considered an excellent match for both families.

Before he introduced Odelia to her new home, Aedgar decided to make some improvements. He lived in the Great Hall of his village, a large and impressive building surrounded by various smaller ones; the kitchen – always kept apart from the main house in case of fire – dairy, laundry, stables, barn, brewery and midden, several small huts where the peasants who worked for the Earl lived, and the whole area encompassed by a wooden picket fence.

There was even a small orchard, several beehives and a vegetable plot inside the fenced enclosure. Just outside was a grassed area where the animals grazed and beyond that the farm spread out through the fields and into the countryside. It all gave a feeling of affluence, permanence and peace.

The Great Hall itself was splendid. The frame, built of oak, soared high into the roof, the beams exposed and covered with thatch. The floor was made of flagstone with a fire pit in the centre, the whitewashed walls made of wattle and daub and windows with shutters that could be opened or closed. A large, heavy oak door made a stately entrance to the building.

Most of the day to day living was done in the Hall. It was where the whole household ate their meals and everyone relaxed at the end of the day. At either end of the building were smaller rooms, the chambers for the family to sleep, part of the improvements that

Aedgar had made. It was to this imposing settlement, improvements finished, that Aedgar brought his bride.

Odelia did her duty as a wife and within a year of the marriage had given him a son. The following year another son was born and after seven years of several failed attempts to have more children, finally gave birth to a daughter, his Rothwynn. Sadly, Odelia died only a few weeks later.

Earl Aedgar promptly hired a wet nurse to care for his baby daughter and then tried to ignore the child. After all, girls were not important until it was time to marry them off to someone who could use their influence for the family's good and advancement. At least that was how it started for Aedgar and Rothwynn. He hadn't counted on his love for this girl child. She became his one weakness.

The years when Rothwynn was growing up were years of relative peace. The country was united under King Edward, known as the Confessor because of his religious piety. There were no famines or rampant diseases to worry the populace and life was easy in the area of England where Earl Aedgar and his family lived; part of the old kingdom of Wessex, situated several miles north of the ancient monument of Stonehenge and near to the old Roman city of Bath.

It was a medium sized settlement comprising the Saxon Hall where Earl Aedgar lived with his family, and the homes and families of the peasants who were his servants and workers. The farm outside the compound spread over the surrounding countryside and supplied them with all their needs.

There was a church with an attached dwelling for the priest, a nearby forest where there was enough deer to provide an abundance of venison for everyone, and a stream that gave them plenty of fresh, clean water.

Rothwynn had her own special place…a small hill just beyond her home that lay between the western wall of the compound and the forest. A very modest hill. It almost looked man made, as though especially for her, at least that's what she thought. It was just high enough that she could see above the roof of the hall and the other nearby buildings to the south and east but not tall enough to see above the trees of the forest on the western side.

It was to this little hill that Rothwynn retreated whenever she needed to be alone, when she was sad or worried or even in especially happy times.

Although Rothwynn was her father's pride and joy, he was a busy man and as she grew older, he hadn't much time for her. With her mother dead and no sisters, her brothers almost grown by the time she was old enough to understand what brothers were, Rothwynn was often lonely.

She spent hours in the kitchens with Werberga, the head cook, who let her help with easy jobs and more complicated dishes as she became more skilled. It was a good opportunity to talk about growing up and girlie things that otherwise Rothwynn wouldn't have had and she valued the experience.

But there were still many hours she spent alone. Sometimes she'd walk and play in the forest, loving the peace and quiet of the place, and learning the ways of the animals that lived there; a fox she came to know well enough that often he would sit and watch her, a badgers sett she found and once saw three young ones playing in the evening dusk. She watched the cheeky squirrels gathering nuts in the autumn and run away as soon as they realised she was there, with their red bushy tails bobbing upright as they went.

One day when she was about seven or eight years old, as she was walking through the forest, she heard a whimpering. Something was in pain so she explored until, following the pitiful cries, she came across a sad sight. A small wolf cub was sitting beside its dead mother. Another two cubs had also died, leaving just the one baby crying, hungry, cold and scared.

As Rothwynn approached she tried to run away but was too weak. Rothwynn picked her up, her heart breaking for the tiny orphan. She removed her cloak and wrapped the cub carefully so she could carry it home.

Wolves were not a popular animal in Saxon society but she couldn't bear to see it suffer. On her journey home she wondered what her father would think.

Well, she already knew if she was honest with herself. He would say it should be killed. But maybe, just maybe, he might let her keep it and try to save its life.

Her father wasn't around when she arrived at the compound so she walked straight to the barn and penned the cub before setting off to find some milk to feed it. She was right. It was starving and greedily lapped up every last drop. Rothwynn was relieved that it was old enough to drink by itself. She spent the rest of the day getting to know Freya, as she named the cub, worried about her father coming home and finding them together in the barn.

It was as bad as she feared. There he stood framed in the massive doorway, impressive in his anger at his daughter. She could feel his fury, but was determined to stand her ground.

The argument was fierce and lasted for what felt like hours to her, but eventually, Aedgar relented after she promised that if she couldn't tame the wolf, Rothwynn would allow the wolf to be destroyed, determined in her own mind that it would never happen. From that day on, Freya, grew and thrived.

Freya grew into the most beautiful wolf. She was strong but gentle and followed Rothwynn around, as if she knew she owed her life to this human. Before long the two were inseparable. Freya slept in Rothwynn's chamber, sat at her feet at mealtimes and when she had her lessons with Father Phillipe.

Aedgar didn't like the animal but soon came to realise that as long as Freya was with Rothwynn his daughter was safe from harm, as the wolf was very protective of his daughter.

In her turn, Freya didn't like very many humans at all, she especially didn't like most men. She tolerated some of the women and children and seemed to like Father Phillipe, the local priest. Next to Rothwynn, her favourite person was Werberga, the cook, who often sneaked tidbits of food to her.

As Rothwynn grew she spent more and more time on her hill, taking Freya with her. It called to her when she was lonely and she'd climb to the summit and sit on the grass overlooking her home and imagine what it had been like in days gone by.

At night she would sometimes wake and as the moonbeams pierced through the shutters she could hear the voices calling to her. Taking Freya with her, she would leave her bed and wend her way to the hill.

Always there was a priest of the old religion. He was tall and very thin, an old man with long white hair and an even longer white beard, dressed in a white robe, with a tall staff in his hand and a gold chain around his neck that had a medallion hanging from it in a curious pattern and shape.

He'd be chanting words she could not understand in a language she'd never heard before and his voice was clear and piercing and very musical. And then, like a puff of smoke, he'd be gone and she was alone again.

It was all very real to her. Sometimes it felt more real than her life in the compound with her father and grandfather.

What surprised her though was the fact that Freya didn't seem to notice anything. It was usual for her to growl if anything was out of the ordinary, if there was a stranger around or a threat of any kind. But if the priest really was there, not just in her imagination, then she knew that he was certainly no threat, but rather a calm and peaceful entity.

Rothwynn and her brothers were taught to read and write by Father Phillipe. He had lately come from

France and before long she was saying French words and phrases scattered among her Saxon English. They learned Latin, more than just was necessary to say the Mass at church, and a little about numeracy.

The lessons were easy for Rothwynn and she hurried through them every day to enable her to return home to ride her pony or play with the latest new born kittens, puppies or chicks, all of them accepted and even mothered by Freya.

Rothwynn had a deep love of music. It was a tradition in her family that after the evening meal was done all the household would gather together in the hall and listen to the songs, ballads and stories of her people. Heroic tales of adventure were told or sung. The exploits of the hero Beowulf were perhaps Rothwynn's favourite, the prince who hunted and killed the evil Grendel, the man eating monster. But the songs were even better.

She had a sweet voice and both her father and grandfather enjoyed listening to her sing and play her lyre. Sometimes her brothers Selwyn and Godric would accompany her on the drums and the flute, then everyone would sing together.

There were many times when she would spend an afternoon with her Grandfather. Rothwynn loved the old man. They had developed a close bond and she often went to him with questions when her father wasn't available.

Somehow during her growing up years she managed to absorb vast amounts of knowledge about the running of the small estate, the ever changing calendar of the seasons influencing the jobs that needed doing on the farm. She learned when and what to plant, about the rotation of crops and how to milk the cows and churn the butter, the use of herbs for healing, and all the other household duties that were necessary for the successful running of a home of their size.

The remaining years of Rothwynn's childhood were happy and carefree. She still had lessons from Father Phillipe and chores to do, but she diligently went about her duties and then was free to do as she wished.

She loved her home and the surrounding countryside, and the villagers were used to seeing her running through the fields or strolling into the forest, always accompanied by her beloved Freya. Life for all who lived in the village was calm and peaceful and Rothwynn wished it could go on like this forever.

CHAPTER 3

The years flew by and Rothwynn grew and turned into a beautiful young woman. When she was almost fifteen her father approached her.

"We need to talk," he told her. "I have arranged a marriage for you. He is a fine young man and will treat you well and make you a good husband."

Rothwyn was horrified.

"But father," she began to remonstrate with him. "I don't want to be married. I don't want to leave you. I want to stay here and take care of you."

"No, child, it's not right. You must wed."

"No, please no," she begged him, her voice soft and pleading.

"There will be no arguments. My mind is made up. The arrangements are all made. His name is Baldric and you will be married in ten days' time. He'll be here in a week. You will make him welcome and you will obey me in this."

"But father," she began again, tears choking her voice.

"There will be no buts." Now her father was getting angry, his voice raised. "This time you will not change my mind."

He was adamant and indeed there was no changing his mind. For the first time in her life she could not bend him to her will. She tried everything; pleading, crying, sulking, and arguing.

It made no difference. For Earl Aedgar it was a good marriage. It aligned his family with another branch of the Saxon royal line. He was nothing if not ambitious and this was something he'd been planning for a long time.

Begetting a girl child had no advantages until she was of marriageable age, then she could be used towards his own ends. Rothwynn had reached that point. Baldric's family would be worth the trouble – important in court circles and very influential.

This time she would be made to obey him. The Earl was beginning to be sorry he'd been so soft with her all these years – now she would learn. He would force her to obey him.

The week sped past until the day was upon them and all Rothwynn's hopes that some event would delay them were dashed. Baldric and his family arrived, the wedding was upon them, and could no longer be avoided. And he was young…very young, not quite thirteen years old. Rothwynn wondered if her father was mad.

"How can you do this to me?" she demanded. "He's still a child! I cannot marry him."

"Of course you can. You will go and live with his family and learn their ways. Then when he is old enough you will consummate your marriage. It's quite a usual thing. Besides, as you are older than him it should be easy enough for you to manage him as you like." He smiled at his daughter. "You've always found ways to make me do your bidding. It should be even easier with Baldric."

He would not be moved, so Rothwynn did the only thing she could think of doing. She went to the church and spoke to Father Phillipe, another man who thought the world of her. She spoke to him of her fears.

"What can I do Father?" she asked tearfully. "I really cannot marry this... this little boy. Besides, from what I've seen of him he's very spoiled and won't make a good husband at all."

"Come then child," the priest responded, "We'll pray for help from the Blessed Virgin. Maybe she will intercede for you." And he led her to the altar where they knelt and prayed together.

Rothwynn didn't understand how she could be helped but she was a virtuous girl and full of faith so she went home feeling hopeful that a miracle would prevent this disastrous marriage.

The day had been one of warmth and sunshine, in great contrast to the way she was feeling inside. She tried to make the best of things, hoping with all her heart and trusting the Blessed Virgin to help her. They celebrated the arrival of Baldric's family with a feast and when it was done the old stories were told as usual.

"Now my daughter Rothwynn will sing to us," Earl Aedgar had announced.

She couldn't refuse. In his present mood her father was not above having her beaten for refusing his request. But no, it was not a request - it was a command that she entertain them, so she obeyed and Aedgar sat there proudly watching her, enjoying the reflected glory of her accomplishments and gracefully receiving the admiration of Baldric's family.

The Hall rang with song until very late. Rothwynn was tired and emotionally exhausted, but when she retired to bed sleep would not come. She tossed and turned and finally climbed from her bed and walked to the window, opened the shutters and was surprised to see how dark it was.

There had been a bright moon earlier in the evening but now it was totally obscured by thick cloud and the atmosphere was heavy and oppressive. She could see lightning on the distant horizon and as she watched, it advanced closer and ever closer, the thunder becoming louder and louder.

Rothwynn had always enjoyed watching storms, as long as she was at home, warm and dry, but tonight it was different somehow. The clouds looked more vicious, more dangerous, the lightning bolts crashing to the earth as though all hell itself had broken loose.

She was frightened and wanted to hide herself in her bed deep under the bedclothes, but found she couldn't move. Instead she stood as though bolted to the floor, terrified yet fascinated at the scene she was watching.

Suddenly, with the loudest clap of thunder she'd ever heard, the lightning struck a building in the compound. Within seconds the whole thing was ablaze, the fire crackling and whistling as it raced through the thatched roof and the dry tinder walls, an easy meal for the flames.

She thought she heard screaming but couldn't tell if it was real, imagined, or if it was the sound of the fire itself, which now had become a living, breathing thing as it roared through the building at tremendous speed. She saw men rush towards the building and realised it was the kitchen that was burning and prayed that no one had been inside – nobody could have survived the holocaust.

She grabbed her cloak and after telling Freya to 'stay', ran outside to join her father and the other men who were standing around helplessly. The thunder storm had passed, retreated as fast as it had arrived.

Now the rain came. Torrential rain. She'd never before seen anything like it. Within seconds she was soaked to the skin. But the rain came too late to help. The building had gone...completely destroyed. Her father had been standing as though turned to stone. Now he rushed into action, barking out orders to his men.

"We must count our people," he informed them. "Is anyone missing? Could anyone have been inside?"

Everyone was accounted for, everyone that is, except Baldric. They hunted for him everywhere. There was no reason he should have been anywhere near the kitchen. They searched all the buildings, then the farm and finally into the forest. By now the clouds had gone and the moon was shining as brightly as before, but it was still dark amid the trees and the undergrowth.

Even with the torches they carried it was hard to see anything. They called out and hunted all night. When the sun arose, still they hunted. The boy's mother, Godgife, was hysterical. Rothwynn made her a drink of valerian and hops to calm her.

Finally, after telling Rothwynn she was a good girl and she would be happy to have her married to her son, she fell into a fitful sleep.

By noon it was agreed that the burnt out remains of the kitchen were cool enough to search the wreckage and there they found what was left of Baldric's body, charred almost beyond recognition. Only the chain around his neck identified him beyond doubt.

His family left, taking home with them not their son's new bride, but what remained of their son's body, Godgife inconsolable in grief for her son.

Rothwynn was also inconsolable, but for a different reason. She believed that she was the cause of the boy's death. If she hadn't prayed for release from the marriage maybe he'd still be alive. She'd never had a prayer answered in such a dramatic fashion but surely it could not be a coincidence? It must be her fault.

And so she too, grieved and tried to bury the feeling of relief she also felt that the marriage would no longer happen. The guilt she felt ate away at her. Gone was the once happy child. She no longer smiled but went about her lessons and her jobs around the house out of habit.

Finally, after a week of deep unhappiness and guilt, she visited Father Phillipe for confession.

"Forgive me Father, for I have sinned. I killed that poor boy," and she sobbed out her heart to the gentle man.

"No, my child. It was not you. You had no control over the weather. It was the storm that killed him."

"But it was my prayers that caused the storm. I wanted him gone and now he is. But truly Father, I did not want him dead."

The good priest hesitated a moment. "There is something you should know, but I cannot tell you. I have heard a confession, so I am not free to speak, but I will ask a certain person to come and talk to you."

And with that Rothwynn had to be satisfied. She went home to wait, but for what? And for whom?

It was late the next day when she and her father had a visit from Werberga, the head cook. At first Rothwynn assumed it was about the new kitchen which had already begun to be rebuilt.

As Werberga approached Earl Aedgar she said, "My Lord, there is something I must tell you concerning my daughter, Willa."

The Earl inclined his head.

"Well, my Lord, apparently she knows something about the young man who died in the fire. It seems she was supposed to meet him, but she is embarrassed to talk about it. Sir, if you could see her and ask questions, she would have to answer you, wouldn't she?"

Aedgar acknowledged the truth of this statement. "Bring her here then. Whatever she knows will help and she must tell us."

So the child was brought to the hall and stood before the Earl looking terrified. She was very young, no more than eleven or twelve years old. She had tears in her eyes and was trembling.

"You need not be afraid," he told her kindly. "We just want to know what happened. You are not in any kind of trouble."

Rothwynn couldn't take her eyes off the girl. She had known Willa since she was born, watched her grow, and thought of her as a sweet child, one of the many children that lived in the compound, the families of the peasants who worked for her father.

Willa stood there, first on one foot and then on the other, her eyes downcast, her hands fidgeting. But she said nothing.

Rothwynn spoke. "Willa, please will you tell me what you know? Your mother has told us that you were to meet Baldric that evening. Is that so?"

The child nodded.

"Why then? Why did he want to meet with you? It is important that we know, so please tell us." She gave the girl an encouraging smile.

Very hesitatingly the story was told...told how Baldric had approached her and asked her to help him. He told her he was to be married and was worried.

"He said worried my lady," Willa said, looking up at Rothwynn. "But he looked scared. I was sorry for him so I said I would help if I could. He seemed so young to be married. I know I would be afraid if I was to be married, and when he asked me to meet him to help him to know what he should do when he was wed, I said I would." She stopped and looked even more embarrassed.

"Go on," Rothwynn encouraged her.

"We agreed to meet in the kitchen after everyone had retired to bed," and she cast a guilty look at her mother as though she'd been caught doing something forbidden. "My lady, really, I thought he meant something to do with the wedding, or at the church or the feast. I didn't know what he… what he was talking about."

"And what was he talking about?" inquired the Earl.

The girl's head hung lower, her voice so quiet they could hardly hear her. "He wanted me to take off my clothes so he could…see…and practice… you know. But I wouldn't so he grabbed at me and started to touch me and…" She could go no further.

"O, my poor child," Werberga said and enveloped her daughter in a voluminous hug. "You should have told me. I would have taken the broom to his backside." Her voice loud with anger.

"Then what?" Rothwynn questioned.

"I hit him on the head with a pan and he fell and I ran away."

"And so I should think," her mother told her, indignant at the way her daughter had been treated. "He deserved it."

"But not to die in the fire," Willa whispered. "And that was my fault."

"Indeed it was not," Aedgar insisted. "It was quite wrong of him to behave in this fashion. You aren't responsible. It was his bad behaviour and the storm that killed him. Not your fault at all. Thank you for coming to tell us. It was very brave of you."

The cook led her daughter from the hall and had been gone for several minutes before Rothwynn's father noticed that she was crying. "What is it child?" he asked.

"I thought it was me. I thought I had killed him. I prayed that something would happen that we could not be wed and the storm came and he died. I thought it was my fault."

"So that is why you have been so unhappy then?"

She managed a nod.

"Well, you can put it all behind you for now, but you know the time will come when you will be wed. I shall choose a husband for you, and you will be married without argument. Only next time I will make sure I choose a man not a boy."

"Why can't I choose for myself?" Rothwynn demanded. "All the girls that live here are allowed to be married to a man they love and want to be with. When the time comes, I want to choose my own husband."

"You are not a peasant and you will be married to a man of your own class, a man of my choosing, a man I consider to be worthy of joining with our family, a man who will be an advantage to us. It is the way it has always been done – love has nothing to do with it. Just be warned girl, if you make it necessary, I will find a man strong enough to break you to his will."

And she knew he meant every word.

Rothwynn had known Werberga all her life. She'd been her friend since she had first visited the kitchens many years ago. In fact, Werberga was not only the head cook of the household, she was also the midwife and had attended Rothwynn's mother when she was born, so Rothwynn had no hesitation in speaking to her about her daughter, asking how she was doing since the death of Baldric.

"Well, my lady, she seems to be coping most of the time, but I know she still feels guilt. She certainly has lost her cheerful spirit."

"Do you think that Willa would be happy if I asked her to be my maid?"

"O, my lady. I think she would be very pleased. She doesn't have enough to do with her time now, just helping me out in the kitchen now and then. And she is a good girl."

Rothwynn smiled her thanks and left to find Willa.

Willa loved her mistress and she enjoyed her new job. Rothwynn didn't really need a maid as she had taken care of herself for most of her life and would have been quite happy to have continued that way.

It seemed to her, however, that Willa needed something to do, so she set about teaching the young girl what her new job would involve. Mainly it was to take care of Rothwynn's clothes and her personal effects. There was a seamstress who did the sewing and made her dresses, but as she was growing up and becoming a young lady, it was incumbent upon her to look and dress that way.

She realised she could do with some help, her own duties around the hall were increasing and it would be good to have someone to assist her.

As for Willa, she'd known Rothwynn all her life and had looked up to her with admiration. To be working for her seemed like a dream come true.

In the beginning she was a little diffident, very unsure of how to behave. Should she curtsy to Rothwynn each time she came into a room? Must she address her as "my lady" all the time? And where would she sleep?

But, no. Rothwynn didn't want anyone curtsying to her or calling her "my lady" all the time, only if they were in public would that be necessary. Alone, she was to be called by her name – Rothwynn.

"But, my lady...I mean...surely that would not be seemly," Willa protested.

"Willa, we are friends, are we not?" Rothwynn answered. "I've known you since you were born. I cannot have you addressing me formally when we are alone."

As for where she should sleep, about a third of Rothwynn's bed chamber had been enclosed for use as a closet and it was there that she kept her clothes in a large chest and there was plenty of room to put a bed. There was also a door giving access to the outside, so Willa would be able to come and go without disturbing her mistress, but be on hand if ever she was needed.

For Willa this was another dream come true – to have her very own space. It didn't matter that it was small. It was all hers and she wouldn't have to share it with the rest of her family.

It didn't take long for them to become adjusted to the new routine and a close relationship developed between them. Neither of them had had a real friend before. Now there was someone to share all their hopes and dreams with, someone who would listen and empathise and understand. Although Rothwynn was three years older than Willa, they were soon sharing secrets and giggling together whenever they had the opportunity, which was usually only first thing in the morning and again before bedtime.

Willa loved to brush Rothwynn's hair. It was a deep honey gold colour and the more it was brushed the more it shone. She also enjoyed taking care of her mistress' clothes. Most of the time Rothwynn wore a homespun overdress, similar to those worn by Willa and the other women, but if there was a special occasion she had some lovely things that were a delight to touch, so soft and silky and such pretty colours.

As Willa brushed Rothwynn's hair, they talked about their day and about boys and men and marriage. Willa wasn't sure she ever wanted to be wed. Having a husband around didn't suit her at all, but if she did, it would not be someone she'd known all her life…who lived around here. No, it would be a handsome stranger. He would ride into the compound on a beautiful horse and sweep her off her feet with his undying love and devotion for her.

"You are so lucky," Rothwynn commented. "You'll be allowed to choose your own husband. My father won't allow that. I'm very much afraid of who he will decide I must marry. His first choice was not a good one and I'm sure his next one won't be any better. I would like to choose for myself."

Once more Rothwynn's imagination took hold. She knew she had to be married, her father had repeatedly told her, so this time she knew he wouldn't change his mind…this time there would be no reprieve.

And so instead of the old priest coming to visit her when she sat on her hill, she would imagine a husband. Not a boy. Maybe someone about the same age as her brothers.

What would he look like? He'd have dark hair. She was sick of all these blonde men around with wishy-washy blue eyes – like her own. She'd rather have brown, big brown eyes, like Father Phillipe.

She liked the good father. Of course, he was old now but he must have looked very nice when he was young. So yes, her husband would have brown hair – not a Saxon then. Maybe French like the priest. She could understand a bit of French so that would be all right.

But she'd want to stay in England not go to France. She'd heard bad things about France from lessons she'd learned from Father Phillipe.

The nearest part of France was now inhabited by the Normans. The French king had been so annoyed with the Vikings constantly attacking their northern coastline that he had ceded it to them as long as they protected the northern coast of France.

For more than a hundred years, these Normans, Northmen, had been living there, had married with the native French, spoken their language, and adopted their customs. But they were still Vikings. Underneath the surface they would always be Vikings – cruel and merciless.

No, she would not live in France. Her husband would have to live here and he would be gentle and kind. She would lie on the grass on top of the hill, her hand gently caressing Freya's head, and dream of this wonderful man who'd come and sweep her away. He'd be tall, handsome, charming and gallant and they would be blissfully happy together. Then dream time over, it would be time for her to go home for lessons or chores.

Soon after the tragedy of Baldric's death Rothwynn's elder brother Selwyn was married and he brought his bride, Annis, to live with them. Rothwynn was excited to have another young woman in her family, at last she had a sister, and life settled down peacefully once again, but not for long.

At the beginning of the year of 1066, the King, Edward the Confessor, died, leaving no direct heir. The Witan gathered and Earl Aedgar left to take part in the important decision making of confirming the country's new king. They'd chosen Harold, son of Godwin and brother-in-law to King Edward. He was the most powerful of the Saxon Earls.

The first few months of Harold's reign were peaceful but they knew it couldn't last. There'd been too many contenders for the throne and there were some who would not accept Harold…who would contest his right to be king.

Spring came and Earl Aedgar announced once more that he had found a husband for Rothwynn. His name was Aelfric. Not her tall, dark and handsome imaginary French lover, but another Saxon.

He was several years older than her and the son of one of Aedgar's friends. More importantly, he was a cousin to the new king; the Earl's ambitions had not abated over the years.

Rothwynn had known of this man all her life and although she'd only met him once or twice, knew that she disliked him. She was afraid of him and thought him a bully; a big man with a temper and a liking for strong drink.

All her remonstrations with her father fell on deaf ears. She confided her fears to her grandfather and he intervened with her father on her behalf, but to no avail. In Aedgar's mind this was a good thing for them all – they would now be closely connected to the kings' family.

Rothwynn would learn. She would get used to being his wife, after all this is what women were for. Once more he was adamant that his rule would be obeyed. For the second time all the joy disappeared from her life, fearing for her future and dreading the time when she would be wed to this man. But before she could be married, or even formally betrothed, war threatened.

King Harold's brother, Tostig, was one of the first to contest the throne. With the aid of Harold Hardrada, king of Norway, he planned an invasion from the north, while to the south, in France, the Normans too were massing to invade, Duke William determined that the English throne belonged to him. King Harold summoned all his Earls to gather their armies and head north to repel the first of the invaders.

Aedgar obeyed his king. He would go and take his brother and both of his sons with him, as well as his small but strong and well trained army, his fyrd, and even the priest. They headed north to join with Harold, leaving behind his aged and crippled father, his daughter-in-law Annis, who was now with child, and had taken to her bed, and Rothwynn, totally unprotected.

CHAPTER 4

*R*othwynn knew they would come. She'd been watching every day for ten days now, ever since the news of the battle had arrived. A messenger had come within forty-eight hours.

They were all dead; her father, her uncle, and both her brothers. All killed in the battle that was to become known as the Battle of Hastings. William the Bastard had landed and the battle for England had been fought on the fourteenth day of October.

King Harold was killed along with all the men of her family, and most of their fyrd. Even Father Phillipe, that sweet, gentle man who had never even raised his voice in anger, and was only there to offer spiritual comfort, had died in the battle.

She watched and waited. No doubt the Bastard would give her home to one of his Norman favourites.

They would probably all be homeless soon; she'd heard that was what had happened in other places.

She'd watched as some of the stragglers passed the compound on their way to somewhere – Wales perhaps – anywhere they could find refuge. They'd begged for food and she'd given what she could, but it wasn't nearly enough.

Before long they'd have no food either and she was responsible for them all; her old grandfather, crippled and bedridden, her brother's wife, Ennis, now heavy with child, and all their servants, mostly women, as the men had all gone to fight and very few had returned. Those that had were wounded, gone into hiding, or had since died.

She didn't know about Aelfric, the man she was betrothed to marry. She should have already wed him but the danger from the north had threatened. He'd gone to fight with his father, a cousin of the King, and their marriage was postponed until the invaders had been repulsed.

But then the Bastard came and with him, the epic march from Stamford Bridge and another mighty battle to face. Her life, as she'd known it for seventeen years, was gone forever. How they were to survive she did not know.

And so every day she scanned the horizon, waiting for them to come, terrified that one day she would see soldiers on the horizon, riding towards her home...to kill every Saxon they found? She dared not even think about their future.

It was early, just past dawn. Once more Rothwynn climbed her hill behind the compound. When she arrived at the top she turned and looked towards the southeast, straining her eyes, looking for any sign of them coming; a glint of sunlight on a helmet, a pennant flying high, or dust churned up from the horses' hooves. There was nothing. It was too early. She would come again in an hour or two. She must be prepared. She must be brave. There were women and children, wounded men and her grandfather, all dependant on her.

It was another two days before they arrived. Rothwyn climbed the hill just as she'd done before, turned to the southeast and saw the sun glinting on the steel helmets. She stood in shock…unable to move… the terror eating at her. Before long they came into full view.

Running down the hill, Rothwynn shouted at everyone to get on with their business as though nothing was out of the ordinary. As though she was hoping that by ignoring the problem, it would go away.

She entered the quiet of the Hall. Her insides quaked like jelly but she was determined not to show it. Taking a few deep breaths and clenching her fists to stop her hands from shaking, she waited until she heard the soldiers enter the compound and dismount from their horses. Their voices were raised, loud and raucous, shouting to each other in French. She heard the call, a refined voice speaking in the Saxon tongue.

Gathering what little courage she could, she walked to the door and stood quietly, a small dignified figure, looking almost lost amidst the Norman soldiers standing around, her hand on Freya's head to stop the wolf from growling, attacking, as she could feel the animal's pent up anger at this intrusion. It had been a priest who had called out and now he approached her and spoke in Saxon again.

"You are the mistress here?"

She heard the surprise in his voice. Bowing her head in assent, she acknowledged, "I am. I am Rothwynn, daughter to Earl Eadgar. This is his land."

"And where is he, child?" the priest inquired.

"He is dead, Father," she explained. "Murdered by the invaders." Raising her little chin in defiance, she glared at the man she assumed to be the leader.

He was standing just behind the priest, impressive looking, stern and determined. Obviously very much in charge. He was tall, yet appeared to be too young to be their leader.

As he returned her glare, she thought he was silently laughing at her, his eyes sparkling with amusement. He spoke to the priest in rapid French, too fast for Rothwynn to understand what was being said.

"Surely you are not in charge here?" exclaimed the priest.

"My grandfather is head of my house," she responded.

"And where is he child?"

"I'm sorry, Father. He cannot be here to speak to you as he is...ill...dying, I think." Her eyes betrayed her and filled with tears as she spoke.

Rothwynn felt herself crumbling. She'd tried to be brave for so long, not allowing herself to cry when she'd heard of her father's and her brothers' deaths. She bit her lip and managed to control the tears. The young man watched her intently then spoke again to the priest.

"I am instructed to tell you that your demesne has been given to Robert de Sellé, who is William, King of England's close aide and friend. This is he."

Robert stepped forward and bowed to her.

"My lady," he said. "I think we have much to discuss. May we go inside?"

Rothwynn was surprised he spoke Saxon. Most Normans could not, but she turned and led the way back into the Hall.

"I doubt you have anything to say to me that I would wish to hear," she stated.

"Maybe not," he agreed. "But there are things that you must know. First, this land now belongs to William, King of England, by right of conquest".

She bit her tongue to stop herself from saying aloud the words she was thinking. So the Bastard's calling himself the King now is he?

Robert went on, unaware of her thoughts. "And I hold it in fief to him now. I am lord and master from now on."

"What happens to my people?" she asked, immediately concerned for them.

"They may stay if they wish, as long as they are loyal to me."

"And the wounded, the few who've returned from battle?"

"They too," he nodded. "I have no wish to turn anyone away from their home."

"Thank you, sir, but I cannot speak for them. I will, however, pass on your kindness, but they may not wish to stay with those whom they blame for the deaths of their husbands and sons."

"They should blame King Harold then," he rebuked, his voice harsh. "He broke his oath when he took the throne of England. He promised it to William."

"It was not his to promise," she replied with spirit. "It belonged to the Witan and they chose Harold, not William."

"We will not argue about this," he declared. "It is all over now. Harold is dead."

"And so is my father, my uncle, my two brothers, and most of our fyrd. For all I know you may be the one who murdered my father. I hope you do not expect me to welcome you with open arms."

"I expect you to treat both me and my men with respect, and I expect you to take me to meet your grandfather."

"He is not well enough," she informed him, her voice breaking.

"Yes, so you said. However, I think he'll want to hear what I have to say to him. I wish to set his mind at ease before he dies."

"Thank you, Sir," she said, managing once more to control her tears and bowing her head to him. "Then if you'll follow me, I'll take you to him."

Despite herself, Rothwynn found she was impressed with the young man. He was certainly an imposing figure and carried himself as though born to lead.

And a fine looking man. Saxon men wore their blonde hair long and often had beards, making them look scruffy. Norman men were clean shaven and wore their hair short. They were darker too, with brown hair and she thought they looked much smarter and neater than the Saxon men, not that she would ever admit it.

So she led him to her grandfather's room, which was a small chamber leading from the end of the hall.

"I will need to remain with you when you speak with him. His sight is no longer good, nor is his hearing, and he may need me to tell him what it is you want him to know."

"As you wish," he agreed as they entered the room.

"It is all right, grandfather," Rothwynn said as she approached the bed. "There is someone here who wishes to speak with you."

The only indication that her grandfather had heard her was a slight movement of his hand. Moving over to the bed she took his hand in hers. His lips moved as though trying to speak. She bent her head close to his to hear his words.

"He wants a priest," she whispered, and sank to her knees burying her head in her hands.

Robert crossed the room quickly and gathered her to him, holding her in his arms as she cried.

"He thinks he is dying," she managed to say between her sobs.

"He shall have a priest then. It will give him comfort." He called towards the door. The priest was standing just outside, "Father Bernard."

Rothwynn moved away from Robert's arms, wiping the tears from her eyes and willing herself to be calm again.

For one brief moment she had felt his strength and longed to lean on him and allow him to take care of her. She needed someone. She'd been alone for too long and didn't know how much longer she could go on.

But no. He was the enemy. There could be no help here. She was stupid to think it for even a second.

"Please, dear God. I really can't take any more. Help me," she prayed silently to herself. "I just want it all to end... now."

Robert's eyes followed her as she walked to the other side of her Grandfather's room. The priest appeared and he and Robert spoke together in French for several minutes.

This time they spoke a little slower and she could understand some of the conversation. Her eyes flashed with fury. Robert looked amused at her reaction then led her from the room.

"Your grandfather needs privacy when he speaks to the priest," he told her. "He may need confession."

As they walked back into the hall, Rothwynn gave him no indication that she had understood what he'd spoken to the priest about, but walked ahead of him with her head held high, although she still struggled with her tears, her fears confirmed by her grandfather. Once he had gone, she would be totally alone in this strange world...all the men in her family gone.

Robert had said that her people could stay, so at least she needn't worry about them. But in a time when women were totally dependent upon the men in their family for protection, her predicament was particularly dangerous.

She walked to the other side of the room away from Robert, embarrassed and trying to ignore him, uncomfortable under his steady gaze. All this time Freya had been walking close by Rothwynn's side and now Robert commented on the animal.

"Is that a wolf?" he asked surprised.

Rothwynn nodded.

"Her name?"

"She's called Freya, but she doesn't like men and she doesn't like intruders, so she may bite you." Rothwynn warned him and thought to herself, I hope she savages you.

Robert knelt down to call her to him. "She'll like me," he responded.

Rothwynn was furious at his assurance.

"Come, Freya." he called and held his hand out to her. Freya moved over to him, smelled his hand and sat there enjoying being stroked by him, looking at him with adoring eyes.

For some reason this betrayal of her precious Freya hurt Rothwynn more than she thought possible. Once more she struggled to control her tears.

Robert leaned against the table watching her every move, admiration in his eyes. She was undeniably beautiful, covered from neck to toe in a blue dress embroidered in gold at the neckline and on the edge of the sleeves, with an underdress of white linen pleated in the skirt and tied at her waist with a gold girdle, although it was unable to hide the lovely curves of her body. White leather slippers were on her feet and a fine white linen veil covering her long flaxen hair that reached almost to her waist, held in place by a circlet of gold.

Her sweet oval face was sprinkled with a handful of freckles across her nose and her deep blue eyes were filled with contempt. He was definitely attracted to her. He was amused by her and impressed by her courage.

Robert could feel the stirring of something...he wasn't sure what. Admiration certainly, but maybe more.

Suddenly he was aware of life returning, and feelings. Were they for her? Whatever it was, whatever had caused it, he realised he wasn't numb anymore.

Father Bernard appeared. "He wishes to see you both." So they returned to his chamber.

Rothwynn immediately ran to his side. "I'm here grandfather," she whispered as she took his hand again.

His voice was weak. "Child," he gasped. "I am dying."

"No, no, you mustn't," she interrupted him, her voice choking with emotion. "Please, please don't leave me."

"It's not my choice, but I don't have long now. I wish to see you safe, child. It is my wish that you marry before I go."

"But..."

"Lord Robert will marry you. He's offered to marry you and take care of you," her grandfather's voice was barely a whisper.

"I'm betrothed already. I cannot marry him."

"I have already given my permission. Aelfric is dead, as are all the others, so your betrothal is at an end."

"No, no, please no," she sobbed.

"Please child, it is my dying wish." His was voice getting weaker. "I want to die in peace. I need to know that you will be all right...safe...that you'll have a home. You will marry him. You will marry him now."

So they were married. Her grandfather watched as Father Bernard recited the words that joined them together as man and wife. The old man was fading but looked peaceful. He took her hand again. "Now I can go, knowing that you will be taken care of."

She bent and kissed his forehead.

"Come," Robert urged. "He needs to rest now," and he led her from the room. "Where is your chamber?" he questioned.

She indicated the other side of her grandfather's chamber. "Through there," she pointed.

"Come then. We have things to do."

"We do? What things?"

"You are now my wife. I wish to bed you."

"No, not now. Please," she begged him, fear of the unknown gripping her, "Not yet, I'm not ready, I don't know you."

Almost against his will, Robert felt himself weakening. His resolve to impose his will on the conquered Saxons, beginning with his new wife, in danger of fading.

"You are my wife and we will consummate our marriage now," he insisted as he led her to her chamber and closed the door behind them, leaving Freya outside.

"Remove your clothes and get on the bed."

The fear intensified. She stood still, unable to move.

"You have a choice. Remove your clothes or I will tear them from you. Which do you prefer?" his voice an icy calm.

Rothwynn glared at him and slowly began to undress, her fingers trembling, making the job difficult. Robert stood and patiently watched her, amusement in his eyes. When she was down to her shift, she stepped towards the bed.

"All of your clothes!" he demanded.

She shook her head. "No, please, no," she pleaded with him, her eyes filled again with tears.

"Now…or I rip it off." He took a step towards her.

As her shift fell to the floor she attempted to cover herself with her hands.

"Put your hands down. I wish to look at you." His voice was harsh so she complied and stood there, not only feeling physically vulnerable, but as though he had also stripped her soul bare.

He stared at her body in admiration. "Yes," he commented. "Very nice. I think I am going to enjoy this very much." And he pushed her down onto the bed.

Later, as he was standing over her straightening his clothes, Robert commented, "So, you weren't with Aelfric then?"

"You already knew that. You don't have to ask again," she retorted.

"Yes, I thought you understood what I told Father Bernard to ask your grandfather."

Her eyes flashed with anger. "And just what made you think that he would know if I had already been with a man?"

"I didn't have to ask him. I knew immediately from your reaction to the question."

"You had no right."

"Indeed I did! I wouldn't take a wife who was soiled."

"You have made very sure that I am now."

"I need a son," he explained to her. "If this demesne is to be secure from Saxon incursion, if it is to remain safely in Norman hands, I need a son.

You will stay there and wait for me to return. I have things to do now, orders to give. We'll have a feast tonight to celebrate our arrival and the coming of the new and rightful King of England. But I won't take long. My steward will carry out my orders and I will be back for more."

She watched him from the bed, anger and defiance showing on her face.

"You know that I can't do anything to stop you," she told him furiously. "But if I were you, I would not turn my back on me or any of my people."

He looked at her for a long minute, his stare frigid. "I will have no hesitation in hanging anyone who tries to harm me or my men – even you." And he turned on his heel and left the room.

When he'd gone, she buried her face in the mattress and sobbed. These Normans were a harsh people, descended from Viking warriors, they had lost none of their brutality. She wept for herself, for her people and for her country, but mostly for the child he was determined she should have.

The past hour had proven to her that he was a hard and passionate man. She was just a body to provide him with an heir and to satisfy his physical cravings. And he was coming back.

CHAPTER 5

*R*obert had managed to arrange for the feast. Rothwynn's servants worked all day to provide them with mounds of food.

She didn't know where it had all come from as their supplies had dwindled. The harvest had been poor this year and most of their provisions had gone with her father and his men. They'd been subsisting mainly on a few vegetables for weeks now and occasionally a little chicken broth. To have venison, pork and plenty of fresh bread and cheese was a rare treat, and it had been many months, even years, since she had seen such a large spread of fruit and cakes; dainty little honey and almond cakes, gingerbread, and tasty cakes made with cheese.

She imagined that Werberga had enjoyed herself immensely in the kitchen with plenty of ingredients to use in her cooking and baking, not having to wonder how she was going to feed the household.

Not only was there plenty to eat, there was also plenty to drink – the mead and the ale that the Saxons drank, and the wine that the Normans preferred. It wasn't long before most of the men were raucous and drunk. Laughter and bawdy jokes bantered to and fro.

Rothwynn sat there hating it all, not wanting to eat any of the delicious food available, knowing it would all taste like straw to her, and wondering what her grandfather could possibly be thinking, what he was hearing now. She'd managed to visit him twice during the day, when Robert had spared her from their bed.

He looked considerably weaker and she knew it wouldn't be long before he died, before he'd be at peace and away from the horror of the Norman invasion of their home and their land. She wished that she could join him. For the first time she was glad that her father and brothers were not here to see what was happening to her and their beloved country.

After a while, Robert stood and put his hand out to her. "Come," he announced. "It's time for us to retire."

"I haven't finished eating," she replied, trying to stall for time.

"Yes, you have." He pulled her to her feet and led her to her chamber. Several of the men called out crude comments as they left. Robert just smiled as he turned to them. "It is your turn next," he informed them amidst loud cheers.

As they entered her room, she asked him, "What did you mean, it's their turn next?"

He shrugged. "There are plenty of women here. My men can have them. Starting nine months from now I want a crop of Norman babies born. Every one of the women who is able will have a child, a Norman child."

She was horrified. "That's rape! You can't allow that! Most of them are married."

"They are widowed," he corrected her. "They will be married again, to my men, and they will bear Norman children. And so will you. Remove your clothes or I will do it for you."

The feast finally ended after hours of boisterous drinking and laughter, but what followed was worse. Rothwynn could hear the screams of the women as they were dragged from their huts or from the Hall and the men took their pleasure. Robert left her for a few minutes and returned with his young squire.

"Where does your maid sleep?" he asked.

"Why do you need to know?"

"I am giving her to my squire," he stated matter-of-factly.

"No, no, please don't. She's hardly more than a child."

"Raoul is hardly more than a child, either," he said, "They will do well together." As he turned to Raoul he announced, "She is possibly in there." and indicated the closet at the end of the chamber. The look on Rothwynn's face told him he had guessed correctly.

"No!" she screamed at him. "Please, no! Leave her be. She's still a child."

"Not for much longer," he replied, showing no compassion and nodded to Raoul. Raoul grinned and entered the closet. Rothwynn heard voices, a scuffle, crying, then voices again followed by silence. She buried her head in the mattress again, sobbing, trying not to hear.

"You are too soft," he told her as he lowered himself onto the bed again. "Be more concerned for yourself." He was right. Soon she was crying for herself.

The next day her grandfather died. Rothwynn was with him at the last and Father Bernard was there to give the old man some comfort. His final minutes were peaceful. He said his goodbye to Rothwynn, closed his eyes and drifted away.

She couldn't be sorry. She was glad that he knew little of what was going on. How she wished she could go with him. How she wished they had all run away into the forest before these Normans had arrived, but that would have meant leaving her grandfather behind and she couldn't have done that.

"I must bear it," she told herself. "I must try to be brave." But it was impossible.

Her grandfather was buried with due solemnity.

Within a few days, the bodies of her father, her uncle and brothers were returned home for burial, too. Her brother's wife, Annis, was soon due to have her child. She heard Robert instructing the midwife.

"If the child is a boy, you will see that it does not live."

"No, no, no," Rothwynn screamed at him again. "You mustn't do this! It's murder," she pleaded as she pummelled him on his chest.

"There must be no one who can dispute my ownership of this demesne," he told her coldly. "It will be done as I say," and he walked away from her quickly, not allowing himself to show his feelings of disgust at what he was doing, what he felt he must do.

Rothwynn didn't know how she survived those first few days and weeks. She tried to be brave, knowing the other women were watching her and would take their lead from her. She'd been the only mistress they'd ever known – at least until her brother had married, but even then they looked to her more than Annis. After all, they'd known her all her life and she was the Earl's daughter.

So she went about her duties; overseeing the women and encouraging them, helping them and working with them. She tried to be cheerful, as she knew, and they did too, that there really was no alternative. These Normans were here to stay.

Rothwynn knew they were lucky that Robert was the one to whom her land had been given. He may be demanding of her when they were alone, in their bedchamber, but in public he treated her with the respect due to his wife. He deferred to her knowledge of the land and was not above asking her opinion about how things should be done, how she would prefer things to be run, where it would be best to place new buildings in the compound.

Not many places had a new master who was sympathetic to the customs of the Saxon people. Horrific tales had reached them about other areas where the people had been brutally treated, so gradually she came to realise that things could have been so much worse and she thanked God for the mercy He had shown them.

Rothwynn was concerned for Willa as she knew that Raoul was visiting the child each night. She could hear quiet voices coming from the closet, but Willa went about her duties as usual. She certainly didn't seem distressed or unhappy.

One day she decided to broach the subject. Willa was brushing Rothwynn's hair, an unusual occurrence these days. Since Rothwynn's marriage to Robert, Willa was not often in her bedchamber, only when Robert was busy on the farm did they have the opportunity to spend some time as before.

"You like Raoul?" she asked, coming straight to the point.

"Oh yes! He's like the man I dreamed of…the stranger who rode into my life and stole my heart away," was the reply.

"He doesn't hurt you?" Rothwynn wanted to know. "I felt so bad for you when Robert decided you two should be together and worried for you."

"There is no need," Willa reassured her. "He's very good to me. That first night…well, he knew I was frightened, so he would not lie with me, we just cuddled and talked. That's all we do each night. We've come to know each other very well. He's a kind and gentle man and quite devout. He wants to marry me. He says we will do things the right way, the way you and Robert did – be married first."

Rothwynn was determined that Willa and Raoul would have a proper wedding. She helped Willa dress and placed a wreath of flowers in her hair. She told Raoul about the "morning gift" that was a tradition in a Saxon wedding and Robert provided the gold for the gift.

Although Saxon weddings were rarely performed in a church, she knew that Normans were more religious in their devotions, so the marriage was performed by Father Bernard in the church and afterwards a feast held in the hall where everyone, from Robert and the bride's parents, down to the farm workers and the Norman soldiers and the children, came for an evening of celebration, and the loving cup was passed around to all.

As a married woman now, Willa and her new husband were given another bedchamber in the hall since most had been empty since Aedgar and his men had left to fight the invaders and Rothwynn's grandfather had died. Once a home was built for them within the compound they would be properly on their own at last.

Several of Robert's men and the Saxon women had already wed, but some of the Normans had wives at home in Normandy and had sent for them, so now there were a few Norman women living in the compound.

Rothwynn had worried at first, not sure how the women would get on together. But she needn't have been concerned as it all seemed to be working out well with a lot of amusement and teasing as both groups – Saxons and Normans – struggled with each other's languages.

Unknown to Rothwynn, Robert was closely watching her. He noticed how hard she worked and how she cared for the women and children. That not only was she beautiful to look at but she had a good heart and kind nature. He appreciated what she was doing to help him, although he realised with wry humour that she wasn't doing it for him but to help her people.

Slowly, first with his eyes and then with his heart, he softened as he watched her go about her daily duties. Before long he was seeking her out among the women or across the room just to look at her, hoping to catch her eye, hoping that she would smile at him or show some sign of recognition, anything to express that maybe she could be thinking of him, that maybe one day she could also love him.

For he knew now that he loved her. He'd admired her from the first moment he saw her standing in the doorway of the hall. She'd looked so alone, so frightened and vulnerable but determined not to show it.

He was in awe of her courage and she had spirit too. It was obvious that she despised the Normans, but for the good of her people and her acceptance that the invading force were here to stay, had decided make the best of a bad situation.

The realisation that he loved her had come an evening about two weeks after his arrival. They'd finished the evening meal, all the household together in the hall as was the custom, when Daegal, Werberga's husband, one of the few Saxon men to return from the battle of Hastings, had asked Rothwynn to sing.

"It will cheer us all up," the old man had announced. "Bring back memories of the good times."

"Ah, so you have talent too, little lady?" Robert had asked her.

"She sings like a bird," Daegal responded for her. "She can play the lyre too," he added rather proudly.

After some persuading she had eventually agreed.

Her voice was sweet and clear. Robert couldn't take his eyes off her. He was completely smitten by her... enchanted with everything about her.

He thought back to the first few days after their marriage, how he'd treated her and was sickened by the thought of his behaviour, ashamed of himself. He'd justified it at the time by deciding that from the first day she must know who was in charge. She had to understand the Saxons were a conquered people – that the invasion was legitimate. Harold had broken his pledge, a sacred vow on holy relics. Now the Saxon people would be punished for this great sin so, he'd punished Rothwynn. From the very beginning she would learn who was master here.

He hated himself for the way he'd treated her. He hadn't counted on falling in love with her and caring for her so much.

Rothwynn was watching Robert too, noticing little things about him that attracted her. He had a kind way with the children, often stopping to talk to them, to ruffle a young lad's hair or to throw a ball as he passed a group playing in the farmyard.

She saw him tenderly pick up a small girl who had fallen and cut her knee. He carried her to the stream, bathed the wound clean and wiped the tears from her eyes, all the while talking softly to her, then sat with her on his lap as he told her a story until she laughed and smiled at him. All better now, he returned the child to her mother. Rothwynn smiled to herself as she watched him.

He joked with his men, complimented the cooks and the maids when a task was well done and worked as hard as anyone on the building projects in the compound. She noticed the way his eyes smiled when he looked at her and how his voice softened as he spoke to her.

He hadn't smiled much when he first arrived, he'd had a faraway look in his eyes, or a look of sadness, but lately his smile had reached those beautiful brown eyes of his. He looked cheerful and sounded happy as though whatever ghost that had haunted him had been vanquished.

Now when he smiled at her she felt herself responding and smiling in return. She couldn't help herself. She realised she was physically attracted to him too. Oh yes! There was much she was beginning to admire about him.

CHAPTER 6

*R*othwynn was amazed at what Robert accomplished over the next few weeks. He was still working as hard as his men, determined to make this venture a success. He even helped with the animals, knowing what to do to help if any were in distress and caring for them if they were sickly. Rothwynn watched him with wonder, feeling drawn to this new side of her husband.

Several of the buildings had needed repair. The repairs were done. The compound was enlarged, and a stone wall was built surrounding it making all safe and secure. New buildings had been erected, housing for his men and their new families and stabling for the horses.

A larger kitchen, a new and bigger dairy, a milking shed and a proper byre for the cattle to winter in, a large stye stocked with a family of noisy pigs, and a blacksmiths forge which was soon in operation day and night producing more armaments for Robert's men.

Another barn had been built to store the supplies that they'd brought with them and more that he expected to be delivered.

Her sister-in-law's baby was born...a girl. She was healthy and Rothwynn thanked God for another mercy. She spent time with Annis and her little niece, enjoying holding the baby and wondering what it would be like to have a child of her own. Robert's baby.

By now the thought of bearing Robert's child was becoming very appealing. Her days were busy with household chores and her nights were filled with Robert. She found herself responding to his touch, looking forward to his lovemaking. He had never been deliberately cruel to her, although he had not concerned himself with her feelings, but now he was gentle and tender, she could tell his feelings had changed.

She knew she was coming to love him, maybe he could love her too. Now it would be different if she was to have a child. By Christmas several of the other women were with child, but she was not.

They celebrated Christmas with a feast, the likes of which they hadn't seen for years. They'd attended Mass at midnight in the little wooden chapel which would soon be enlarged with stone walls and a slate roof. Things were changing and it was difficult for Rothwynn to disapprove these changes. She couldn't remember a time when her people had been better housed and better fed.

As Rothwynn went about her daily duties, she noticed that the Saxon women seemed content with life now, especially those who were with child. Was it just because life was more comfortable now? They were no longer constantly hungry – as they had been in the weeks since the Saxon men had left for war and before the arrival of the Normans. And their new husbands, were they treating them well?

Of late she had noticed that Robert was treating her kindly, and considerately in their bed. She had come to look forward to their lovemaking. It was also obvious to her that his men respected and looked up to him. She had to admit he was a good leader.

She no longer thought of Aelfric, except those times when she was filled with relief that her marriage to him had never happened. She'd been betrothed to him but had never really known him. Aelfric was not someone she had cared for, or wanted to marry.

She could never forget how she had felt about him, how scared she was of him, remembering the time she'd begged her father not to force her to marry him and had never accepted the idea of becoming his wife. She had even berated herself once or twice for not marrying Baldric when she had the opportunity - a boy yes, but she thought she could have handled him.

But now, looking around at what had been accomplished in the short time that Robert had been in charge, she came to realise that things for her were much better than they could have been.

Aelfric had been a bully, a big burly fellow with no consideration for anyone but himself. He had a foul temper which he never tried to control, especially when he was drunk. If the stories she'd heard of him were true, he was frequently drunk.

And was it true that he'd been married to a young girl who'd died in mysterious circumstances? Rumour said so, said that she'd been so frightened of him that she'd run away, run to a man she'd loved and Aelfric had followed her and killed them both.

But surely her father wouldn't have betrothed her to a man like that, would he? She couldn't help but wonder at her father's motives in wanting her to wed him.

Robert was the complete opposite; kind, gentle and thoughtful with everyone around him, especially the children. Not perhaps to start with, at least not with her. But now – now it was so very different.

Now she thought she was falling in love with him. If he entered the room, she'd feel her heart start to pound a little harder, and sometimes it felt like she had butterflies inside and knew she was blushing. Was this love? She had certainly never felt like this before.

And maybe even more importantly, she trusted him, knew that she would trust him with her life. At last she had someone she could lean on, someone who would take care of her.

Her grandfather had always been a good judge of character. He'd been right. At long last she felt safe.

They survived the winter months well and in the early spring work on the land began, preparing the soil for planting. Everyone worked well together, almost eagerly, Robert's men being used to farm work as her father's fyrd had been, mostly farm workers called to arms only in time of war or danger. Robert himself helped with the lambing, easing many new born lambs gently into the world and did more than his share of the labouring when he deemed it necessary.

Rothwynn had been married for five months and was still not with child. She expected that Robert would be angry with her but so far there had been no reproach. Even her maid, Willa, was to become a mother and had blossomed into an attractive young woman.

Rothwynn wondered what would happen to her if she were barren. Robert said he needed a son. Would he put her away, maybe into a convent somewhere and marry again? Someone who could bear him a child, the son he craved?

Worrying about it helped her to realise that she longed for a child too…Robert's child…his son. She hated the thought of someone else taking her place, not just as mistress of this place – her home, but in their bed, too.

At last she knew they belonged together, they two were as one, complementing each other, working together to make a success of this endeavour. The realisation allowed her to look on him differently; happy to see him when he came in from the fields where he'd been working with his men; happy when he took her in his arms and kissed her; happy with him in their bed.

She admired the way he'd taken charge of her home and turned it into a successful enterprise. They had plenty of food and were planning for the future, making improvements all the time.

She hadn't known a time when things had been run so well. Everyone appeared content, even the children who were learning their letters from Father Bernard. The hard work was almost over. Now the compound was secure, all safe within its walls. The little stone church was growing, too. It would be finished by the summer.

One evening as they went to bed, she ventured to speak with him. "I'm sorry that I have disappointed you."

"You haven't disappointed me. I enjoy our times in bed together."

"But it has been unsuccessful. I am still not with child."

"We will just keep trying until you are. I've heard that sometimes it can take a while, especially for a first child. It will be the most pleasurable task I have ever had." he said with a smile that, once more, made her heart beat faster.

"I worry that I may be barren," she whispered so softly that he hardly heard her. "So many of the women are with child now. It seems you will get your crop of Norman babies that you wished for, just not your own son."

"I will get a son, and by you, when God wills it," he replied as he caressed her face gently. "Don't worry my love, it will be all right."

"Could we have Father Bernard bless our marriage bed?" she suggested.

"If you think it would help, I will ask him tomorrow. But we'll make an extra effort tonight." And he pulled her towards him kissing her tenderly.

The next day Father Bernard blessed their marriage bed.

CHAPTER 7

For weeks, while Robert was watching Rothwynn, he noticed that sometimes she wandered out of the compound for an hour or two. He wondered where she was going but was loth to follow her, so he waited patiently and hoped she would eventually tell him what she was doing when she left.

As he felt that their relationship had begun to change, one day he risked asking her. He'd been in the stables when he saw her pass by on her way out of the compound, taking Freya with her.

He called out to her. "Rothwynn, are you busy?"

She turned and smiled at him. "No, I'm just going for a walk to clear my head a little. Would you like to come? Do you have time to come with me?"

"I would like that more than anything." So he joined her and they left the compound together and he took her hand as they walked.

"I've noticed that you like to slip off from time to time," he said. "Do you go anywhere special?"

Looking up at him, she smiled again.

"I'll show you," she admitted, as they walked towards the hill that overlooked the compound and the surrounding area, the wolf bounding ahead, leading the way as though she knew exactly where they were going.

The climb to the top was not far, but quite steep and it was several minutes before they reached the summit and as they climbed she shared her childhood experiences.

"We used to roll down the side and have races to see who could reach the bottom first. And sometimes we'd picnic on this ledge."

Robert could see where she meant. A section of the hill looked as though it had been levelled off before rising again.

When they reached the top, she exclaimed, "I love it up here. Just look at the view."

Robert had been there before, just for a cursory inspection when he first arrived, and had noticed it as a good lookout point but hadn't been back since. Now he looked around him properly.

First, below to the Hall and the other buildings where he could see people going to and fro about their business and the children playing. He let his eyes follow the stream as it flowed out of the village towards Castle Combe and then his eyes wandered farther north up to the Cotswold hills. Next he turned towards to the southeast and noted he could see for miles over the flatter landscape.

Finally, in the other direction, west, the forest was blocking his view, but the trees had a beauty and feeling all their own. He knew they hid a myriad of tiny lives; animals big and small, birds, insects, a whole world of its own. It all felt very peaceful and something more.

"I can see why you come here," he agreed softly. "It's breath-taking, isn't it? It has a feeling, as though it has a secret of its own."

"You can feel it too?"

He nodded. "Oh yes, it is indeed very special."

"I call it my special place," Rothwynn told him. "I think that once upon a time in the dim and distant past, in the days of the old religion perhaps, it was a holy place. Sometimes when I come here there is a mist swirling around and I think I can hear something, a murmuring as though someone is talking very softly. It isn't frightening, it's somehow...comforting, it's serene and almost magical."

She hesitated. "It's as though I can feel a presence...a very kind benefactor, someone who is here to protect me. A guardian angel perhaps." And she smiled at him, hoping he would not think she was being fanciful. "I come here whenever I need comfort or even to celebrate something special, and I always find what I need. I can find peace here."

Robert understood what she meant. There were a few trees at the summit, ancient yews. They had been planted in a semi-circle, but so many years ago that they had grown together forming an arbour, the opening facing the east towards the rising sun. Obviously at one time they'd been specifically planted there - for a purpose. In the centre of the opening was a large stone set into the ground as though it had been the foundation for something larger.

"I believe that once there may have been an altar there," Rothwynn explained. "It's been said that the old religion practiced sacrifice but it doesn't seem like a place of death to me. It feels like a place where life was celebrated."

He couldn't help but agree. The atmosphere was almost tangible. He felt it soak into his very being. He stood behind her and encircled her in his arms as they gazed into the distance.

"Thank you for bringing me here and sharing your special place with me. Would you mind if I come here from time to time?"

"Of course not. This all belongs to you now."

"But I can't encroach here without your permission – I would feel as though I was intruding."

"You are welcome here," she told him with a smile. "I can feel the approval of the spirits that belong here, whatever or whoever they are." There was a pause as they both stood, unwilling to break the spell. She turned to face him. "I have a confession to make," Rothwynn admitted. "It may sound silly, but I met you here before."

"I don't think so. I've only been here once before and I was alone."

"No, you don't understand. Long ago. Before you even came to England. A couple of years ago. You were here with me."

He stared at her, not understanding and with a quizzical look on his face. "You're right, I don't understand."

"Well, it's hard for me to explain." There was a long pause while Rothwynn tried to gather her thoughts.

"Sometimes, on very lonely days, I would come here and try to imagine what it would be like in the old days, the days of the old religion. There was a priest, an old man. Oh, I know I only imagined him but he was very real to me. I knew everything about him; how he looked, the sound of his voice, the way he was dressed. And then about two years ago my father betrothed me to a young boy."

"This was before Aelfric?" Robert inquired.

She nodded. "Yes. His name was Baldric. He was about twelve years old, a child, and I...I was so unhappy I went to see Father Phillipe and we prayed that it wouldn't happen and then...well, he died, rather horribly, and it was my fault, or I thought it was my fault. It wasn't, I understand that now, but I didn't then and I was very unhappy and I came up here and I met you. I'm sorry, that was very garbled."

"No, tell me."

"The old priest..."

"Yes?"

"Well, like I said, he wasn't real, but to me he was. And then there was you, and you weren't real either, but to me you were. I saw you, only I thought you were French, not Norman."

"You're sure it was me?"

"Oh yes. When you came, I mean were really here… after we were married…" She didn't know how to go on.

"I'm sorry, so very sorry. I know I treated you badly."

She shook her head. "No, I understood that, at least, later on I did. But I recognised you, from my dream, if you could call it that. I knew it was you, just a few days after we were married. When we buried my grandfather and you were so kind. Remember?"

They had stood side by side at the edge of the grave and Rothwynn had felt so totally alone…completely abandoned, the last of her relatives gone. She was left with this stranger, this man who was her husband, her future stretching out before her, unknown, unwanted. She'd never known such deep unhappiness or loneliness.

And then Robert had placed his arm around her and held her close and she'd leaned on him and felt his strength. It was the dream come to life.

"I'll take care of you," he'd said. "I promise I will take good care of you, keep you safe and try to make you happy."

She'd looked up at him and suddenly she realised she'd seen him before. She already knew him.

"It's you," she'd murmured, with wonder in her voice, nothing more than a whisper. "It really is you." That was when she knew that it would be all right, her future safe with this man.

"It shocked me at first, that I would feel that way," she told him. "You weren't French at all, but one of the hated Normans. But then I loved you and it didn't matter because it was you all the time."

"Well, I didn't know you before," Robert admitted. "But although I didn't realise it at the time, I loved you the minute you walked through the door, the first moment I saw you, the most beautiful girl I had ever seen.

"And so full of courage. Your world had just come crashing down, ended really, and you stood there all alone. You looked so young and vulnerable and tried so hard to not show how frightened you were. And I've loved you just a little more every day ever since. I will love you forever. You know that, don't you?"

She sighed. "Oh yes, we'll be together forever. Promise me?"

"I promise." There was one more thing he wanted to know. "Do you still see the old man? The priest?"

She shook her head. "Not since the day my father left. I came up here to watch them go and...and I was praying in my heart that all would be well with them."

She had trouble saying the words, and could feel the pain of it all over again so she paused before she continued. "They had to go north to fight Tostig and his army and we knew that William was waiting in Normandy to invade, so I knew...I knew that I might never see him or my brothers again."

A small sob escaped her. "I knelt in the grove and prayed out loud to ask God to protect them all and bring them home safely to me. But I think I knew I would never see them again. I couldn't stop myself from crying." She looked up at Robert and tried to smile.

"Like now," she said as the tears came, and after a pause, continued. "And suddenly he was there, the priest, he stood in front of me and I felt him put his hands on my head almost like a blessing, as though everything would be all right. And it was, eventually, because you came. But I haven't seen him since. It's as though I don't need him anymore because I have you now."

He held her closer and kissed the top of her head. "I hate to think what I would do without you," he confessed. "You are the light of life." He took her hand.

"Come," he said, and led her over to the grove of trees and they stood, one either side of the stone embedded in the ground, hands entwined where the altar used to be. He looked lovingly at her. "I pledge to you now, in this holy place and as God is my witness, that we will be together forever, that I will love you and care for you until the end of time and beyond."

Then he took her in his arms and kissed her tenderly.

She knew that whatever happened, she was safe in his love and he in hers. They stood there a while longer, unwilling to break the spell until Rothwynn reached up with her hand and caressed his cheek, and sighing again said softly, "I think it's time to go home. I have things I must do, and I expect you do to."

He put his hands to her face and traced her cheeks with his fingers then lifted her chin and kissed her once more, longingly and lovingly, then took her hand and they walked back down the hill, Freya once more leading the way.

CHAPTER 8

The trouble began soon afterwards, hardly noticeable at first. A few hens disappeared, a cow from outside the walls of the compound, and then some supplies from the barn. Robert ordered a watch kept and the thieving stopped.

Then one of the guards was attacked and badly injured as he was patrolling outside the boundary of the compound. A few workers in the fields were also attacked, several of them hurt, Robert ordered the guard doubled. Some of the Saxon women grew afraid.

What if their menfolk had not been killed on that fateful day in Hastings but had returned from the battle and were now living in the forest? Would they expect them to give up this new life of plenty? Would they be angry that they were living as wives to Norman men? Giving birth to Norman children? Perhaps angry enough to drag them away to live as outlaws in the forest or even kill them?

Rothwynn was walking through the compound one morning and heard a few of the women speaking, not close enough to hear what was being said, but the name "Aelfric" was mentioned.

She was alarmed and she thought they could be right. Aelfric. She'd been frightened of him before but now she was terrified. She explained her fear to Robert, and he tried to calm her fears. He held her close to him, trying to bring her some comfort.

"We will catch whoever is responsible," he told her, "Aelfric or someone else. They won't bother us again."

He immediately dispatched a patrol through the forest to hunt down the displaced and homeless vagrants that lived there. They caught some and hanged a few, those they determined were the perpetrators of the theft, as a deterrent to any other outlaws. Stealing food to live was one thing, but attacking and injuring the guards was something he could not allow. But there was no sign of Aelfric.

And then one day she saw him...or thought she did. A blonde giant of a man standing in the distance on the edge of the forest. He seemed to be watching her but when she turned and stared at him he melted into the trees. Was he really there or had she imagined it?

Rothwynn tried to put it out of her mind but it happened again and this time she was certain. Aelfric! What did he want? This had never been his home so what was he doing here?

Unless he was coming for her, but why would he want her now? Robert had told her he wouldn't have a soiled wife. She was sure that Aelfric would feel the same, and he would consider her well and truly soiled now.

If he captured her what would he do with her? Kill her for forsaking him? She'd had no choice then but he wouldn't consider that. Once more she mentioned it to Robert and although he thought she had possibly imagined it, he promised to be more vigilant.

Now that she'd been with Robert for the past six months, she knew she would rather be dead than with Aelfric. She would kill herself if he caught her.

Several days passed and there was no more sign of Aelfrc. Things were peaceful once more. Many other parts of the country were not nearly so fortunate. Rumours swirled of rebellions that King William had put down with the utmost ruthlessness.

Hundreds, maybe thousands, had been killed or left homeless and without means to support themselves. Many of these poor souls roamed the countryside seeking sustenance and shelter, most of them not finding it and dying by the wayside or descending into robbing and plundering.

Rothwynn realised how lucky they were to have Robert as their new master. He was firm with discipline and she'd been angry with him at the beginning when he'd insisted that his men and the Saxon women should marry and produce children that were neither Saxon nor Norman.

He'd hoped that it would avoid the kinds of problems that were appearing in most of the country. Only time would tell if he was right.

Rothwynn finally was with child. She was sure she even knew when she had conceived. It was the day that Father Bernard blessed their bed. Robert had informed her they would spend the day there and for her, it had been a day of wonder and great tenderness, she felt at last that she could express her love for him in this physical way. Afterwards, he'd softly caressed her face and held her gently in his arms.

"Well, that was certainly worth waiting for, wasn't it?" he asked. "You are very precious to me. You do know that, don't you?"

"You mean, more than just someone to bear your sons?" she responded teasingly.

"So much more. I love you. I thank God every day for giving you to me."

The tears in her eyes were at last tears of happiness, no longer of pain or fear.

She learned a lot about Robert from Father Bernard. He'd said Robert was an aide and friend of the Bastard King, but it was his father who had been the King's friend. William had given preference to Robert because of his father.

The King's closest friends had been awarded much larger and more important land holdings than Robert. His endowment was small in comparison to others but he ran it well, his dream of having his own land and home finally realised, and it seemed to be successful and the people content.

One evening as they prepared for bed, Rothwynn had asked Robert how he knew the Saxon tongue and he'd told her that his mother was Saxon. She'd been forcibly taken from a coastal town in Wessex. He didn't know where exactly.

"One day I hope to find her home and learn about her family," he told her. "It's been a dream of mine ever since she died."

Rothwynn's heart was touched, "Do you have any idea where her home was?" she asked quietly.

"All I know is that it was on the coast, further west than here, near some red cliffs that led down to the sea," he smiled as though he were listening to his mother's voice telling him about her childhood home.

"How old was she?" Rothwynn wanted to know.

"She was about twelve," was his response.

She'd been sold to his father who'd bought her as a slave but when she was about sixteen he had married her. She'd borne him five children - three boys and two girls, Robert being the second son. His older brother, Gilbert, was to inherit their lands in Normandy. His younger brother, Armand, had gone into the church, and he'd been left to make his mark in the world with his sword, which he'd done. He informed her, with a smile that he wished to have six children, one more than his father had.

"It may happen sooner than you think," Rothwynn smiled at him. "Beginning sometime in the New Year."

Robert gazed at her in wonder as he realised what she was telling him she was with child. Overjoyed with the news that he was going to be a father, he twirled her around, the excitement showing on his face as he exclaimed, "I'm going to have a son!"

"What if it's a girl?" Rothwynn asked cautiously.

"Then I will love her because she will be like her mother," he grinned. "But it is a boy, I just know it."

Rothwynn estimated that the child would be born sometime in the New Year. But before the month of May was out they knew they were going to have trouble.

The weather had been kind to them and they'd managed to finish all the spring planting, made repairs to the dwellings, and even replaced the thatch on the Hall. The little stone church was almost completed, the future looked promising. It had been peaceful for a couple of months so they were not nearly as vigilant as they should have been. Then it happened. They were attacked.

The first warning came from Freya. She had been sleeping at the foot of Rothwynn's bed. She raised her head and a small rumble emitted from her throat, gradually getting louder. Robert was up in a second.

"What is it?" Rothwynn asked sleepily.

"I'll go and see," Robert told her, "Stay there, I'll be back as soon as I take care of what is bothering her."

Hardly had Robert left than a bloodcurdling scream shattered the silence. Now Freya was at the door barking loudly, the fur on her back standing on end and more screams were heard as the intruders swarmed over the wall surrounding the compound, viciously attacking anyone that got in their way. They carried torches and soon had some of the buildings blazing, creating more confusion.

Acrid smoke filled the air making it difficult to breathe and to see. The Norman soldiers made a valiant attempt to protect the compound, fighting for their lives and for the lives of their families, managing to drive the invaders off but at great cost.

The guards were found with their throats cut. Some buildings burned to the ground. They found the bodies of five of the raiders, and knew many more had been wounded, a quarter of Robert's fighting force were also dead or injured, a couple of the women were dead too. Freya had been killed trying to protect her mistress. And Rothwynn was gone.

CHAPTER 9

*R*othwynn awoke to find herself bound hand and foot and lying in the back of a wagon which was bouncing along a forest track. She thought she'd been frightened when she was forced to marry Robert, but this was beyond anything she could have imagined.

Terrified, her head was pounding from where she'd been struck. As she tried to move and wriggle her hands free the rope cut deep into her wrists. Everything was so dark she couldn't make out where they were. She heard the men talking as they rode through the undergrowth.

Saxons. She'd thought they were and now she knew. This was too well planned to be just a few stragglers…a few starving men searching for food. They'd found a leader.

They continued on, she estimated about half an hour, before they stopped. Distraught at the death of Freya, she could still hear the ferocious growl of fury as the animal leaped at her attacker and sank her fangs deep into his arm, still hear Freya's yelp of pain as she was clubbed over the head and beaten to death. Tears were streaming down her cheeks knowing how much she would miss her beloved pet who'd been her constant friend and much loved companion for many years.

Now bumped and shaken, tossed and turned with the rough movement of the wagon, Rothwynn was even more scared for her baby. And then all was still. There was raucous laughter and a man's voice barking out orders, then quiet as they obediently went about their duties.

Footsteps came towards the wagon and before she realised what was happening, someone was dragging her out by her feet, undoing the ropes that had been restraining her and lifting her down. Her captor turned her around to face him. Aelfric. Trying to hit him, he caught her wrists.

"Ah, no. I don't think you will do that," he laughed at her.

"What do you think you are doing?" she hissed at him.

"Reclaiming my property."

"I don't belong to you."

"Yes, you do. You were promised to me and I will have you," he interrupted her.

"No!" she screamed. "I'm married now. I will never be yours!"

"You were betrothed to me first. You are mine. And I will have you," he repeated.

"No! No! No! Never! You can try to keep me here but I will not belong to you."

"You think you belong to that Norman pig? Let him try to get you back and he will die."

The thought filled her with dread. She knew Robert would try. She had to think. Her mind was in turmoil but she had to think clearly so she would know what to do. She had to get out of there.

She'd lived in the area all her life, she was familiar with the forest, knowing every inch of the place. That would give her an advantage over Aelfric. He was a stranger here.

But first she had to find a way to escape. They mustn't know she was thinking she could get away. If they thought she was compliant, maybe they wouldn't guard her as closely. Tied by her ankle to a tree, she was hobbled like a horse and there was nothing she could do now but bide her time and take her chance when it came.

It came sooner than she thought. Aelfric was determined to claim her as his and if she wouldn't come willingly he certainly wasn't averse to rape. In fact he'd enjoy it and was eager for her. He lived rough now, and so could she.

"Come Rothwynn," he demanded as he untied her and grabbed her wrist, dragging her behind him. "You should have been mine a year ago. We didn't have a marriage but I will bed you anyway…now." And he threw her to the ground.

"Leave me alone," she screamed, terrified of what was to come.

"I'm sure your Norman pig does this to you all the time," he sneered. "Now you can learn what it's like to have a Saxon instead."

He went to lie down on top of her, but Rothwynn quickly rolled away from him and managed to grab the knife out of his belt.

Pointing it at him, she threatened, "If you touch me, I will not be afraid to use this."

He laughed. "I'm not frightened of you little girl. You won't be able to strike me with that knife."

"Not you," she informed him as she held the knife to her throat. "I will kill myself before I let you touch me."

"You wouldn't."

She heard the doubt in is voice.

"Oh, yes I would," she declared. "I have a husband and I will be faithful to him. If you try to touch me I will do it." Her voice held firm.

Aelfric hesitated, just long enough for her to jump up and run. She ran and ran until she felt her lungs were bursting. She heard him pounding after her but she knew her way through the forest.

Gradually he fell behind as she weaved in and out of bushes and trees, first going to the left and then to the right, twisting and turning back on herself until she was sure she'd lost him. She found an old hiding place she'd played in as a child and lay curled up and still until all sounds behind her had gone. Then she crept out very quietly and slowly made her way towards home.

They'd been looking for her. Rothwynn saw them in a clearing in the distance and it gave her renewed strength. She ran towards them and straight into Robert's arms.

"Don't let me go, please hold me," she begged him when she could speak, her voice trembling with relief.

"I will always keep you safe," he promised her as his arms tightened around her. "I will never let you be afraid again." He picked her up in his arms and carried her home.

She slept for hours. She'd lost her baby. Whether it was the jarring ride on the wagon or being thrown to the ground, she didn't know what had caused it, but it was over. When Rothwynn awoke Robert was there and he encircled her in his arms. "I thought I'd lost you," he whispered. "I don't want to live without you."

"I lost our baby," she sobbed into his shoulder, reliving the moment when she realised it had happened. She had wanted to call him back but found she couldn't speak. She removed her bloodied clothes and fell into bed, exhaustion finally taking over.

Now Robert confessed, "It was my fault. I relaxed our guard. It was my fault. And now I'm going on a manhunt. I will get him and I will hang him."

He kissed her on her forehead before letting her go and moved to leave the room. "Robert." She stopped him and he turned back to her.

"He didn't touch me. He wanted to but I threatened to kill myself. That's how I got away."

He smiled at her and then was gone.

They were gone for three days, the worst three days of Rothwynn's life. She'd lost her baby, her precious Freya too, was now gone. She worried the whole time;

worried they wouldn't find who they were looking for; scared they could be hurt; and worried that Robert wouldn't come back to her.

It was late in the day when they returned tired, hungry and dishevelled, but successful. Their prisoners, ten of them, were being dragged behind the horses. Some of Robert's men had been injured, but fortunately, not too badly.

They seemed happy to be home and their wives were happy, hugging each other, relieved and delighted to be together again, not the least of them, Rothwynn. She was surprised at her reaction upon seeing Robert. The joy she felt that he was safe and had come home to her.

But her reaction to seeing Aelfric was one of fury. She hoped that Robert would hang him. He'd tried so hard to destroy all the good that had been done, and was responsible for so many deaths and so much destruction, as well as the death of her much longed for baby.

She wasn't disappointed. They hanged all ten of them. Aelfric had spat at her.

"Rot in hell," she snapped angrily then turned and walked away, not wanting to watch the hangings.

CHAPTER 10

The attack on the compound meant that Robert's plans for the future were delayed in order for the many repairs to be made. Several buildings were damaged beyond repair and they'd lost others in the fires. The work on the church halted for a while and then it was harvest time and everyone was required to help.

Before long, the new barn was filled with food, enough to see them through the winter. The work on the church resumed and when it was finally finished and ready to be dedicated, as a compliment to his wife, Robert had it dedicated to Our Lady.

With the work on the compound complete and peace settled on the community, Robert confided in Rothwynn that he would like to try to find his mother's home. Armed with the small amount of knowledge he had of her background, they set off on a pilgrimage to the south coast, leaving the steward in charge of their home and taking a handful of Robert's men with them as an armed escort – caution was still required when travelling, especially for Normans. A lone Norman travelling would be easy prey for an outlaw to ambush and kill.

It would take many years before the Saxons were subdued. But he made sure that the compound was well guarded, not wanting to return and find they'd been plundered again.

They set off early on a crisp and clear morning, the sun just peeping over the horizon. Rothwynn was excited to be going on this expedition with Robert and felt that it was the beginning of a new chapter in their lives.

He'd confided so much of his life to her, the deep feelings he had for his mother and her family background, how he'd felt when she died and how he'd longed to come to England and find her home. He'd waited so long for this day to come.

Now it was here and he was apprehensive about the outcome of his search.

They headed directly south until they reached the coast and then turned west. With the descriptions of Aerlene's home, the beach where she had played as a child and the cliffs towering above, Robert hoped he would recognise something...anything that would say to him: This is it!

"What are we looking for?" Rothwynn asked.

"Well, there's a river that runs into the sea, a small estuary. And the beach is pebbled, at least at the top end, the sand is covered by the sea when the tide is in.

"But the main thing is the red cliffs. She said some are very high, but where she lived they were at least climbable with a footpath leading from the beach. It's a bay, so you can't see all along the coast, as a point obstructs the view."

They travelled for three days along the Wessex coast, further and further west, until the fourth day early in the morning, he was sure he'd found it. There was the river joining the sea and there were the cliffs exactly as she'd described them, almost red and reaching high above the beach.

"Here!" he shouted excitedly. "I'm sure this is it. She said the cliffs were red." His eyes followed the cliffs until they reached the point. "Yes, I'm sure this is the right place."

They made their way towards the cliffs hoping to find a way through. The village Robert was looking for was inland a mile or so.

After searching through the undergrowth they found a footpath, not too steep but difficult to spot as it was so overgrown. They managed to force their way along by riding in single file, Robert leading the way.

They hadn't gone far when they found signs of civilisation, but no sign of life. A few abandoned houses, tumbling down, the thatch long gone and walls crumbling, everything overgrown with weeds and brambles. It looked as though it hadn't been inhabited for many years.

They alighted from their horses, tethering them safely as they began to explore the ruins, finding evidence of several houses that had almost disappeared. It had once been a thriving community. What had happened here? Could this be the place? Could the raiders who had taken Aerlene have reached here and taken everyone? Or had they all been killed or somehow escaped? The questions filled his mind. He had to know.

They travelled further inland, following another overgrown pathway between the trees and dense undergrowth, until in the distance they saw smoke rising, reaching for the sky. Another thirty minutes and they arrived at a small village. Before they had a chance to dismount, they were surrounded by a group of people, ragged and surly. The weather was beginning to chill, the mornings frosty and cold but the children were barefoot, their clothes thin and dirty, the adults belligerent.

"Who are you and just what are you doing here?" demanded the one who looked to be their leader.

"I'm searching for my mother's family," Robert told them. "She lived near here as a child and was taken by Viking raiders many years ago. I'm hoping to find someone who can tell me what happened to her village."

"You're a Norman," the man accused him. "We don't want any more of your kind here. We already have enough Normans." He spat on the ground.

"But I am not," Rothwynn interrupted. "I am Saxon. This man is my overlord now. It is sad that we have been invaded by these Normans but it is done now and things are never going back to the way they were. It is no longer just a Saxon country. We have to learn to live together."

She paused for a moment. "You have a Norman overlord here?" she asked.

"Indeed we do," was the man's answer. "And he's a harsh master." He muttered some insulting words under his breath. "We don't need no more of the bastards here."

"I am not staying," Robert reassured him. "I just want to find someone who remembers what happened to the village by the coast, the abandoned one a few miles to the south of here."

"That might be old Wirt, he's the oldest around here, he may know," the man told him somewhat begrudgingly. "But he won't want to talk to you and he may not remember anyway – his memory's not so good now."

"Please, where is he? I must at least try."

Robert and Rothwynn dismounted from their horses, handing the reins to their escort, then they were led to a very dilapidated hut with some old sacking in the doorway.

"Hey Wirt," shouted the man. "There's some Norman who wants to talk to you so you'd better come out."

They heard some shuffling, coughing and wheezing and within a few minutes an old man appeared. Not much more than skin and bones, he was almost bent double, fingers knotted and twisted with age, his hair white, sparse and sticking up on end. He leaned heavily on his stick and as he looked up at them they saw his eyes were almost blind.

"Your name is Wirt?" Robert asked him kindly.

The man nodded. "This man's not a Norman," he announced, his voice surprisingly strong for one who looked so old. "He speaks Saxon."

"My mother was Saxon," Robert explained. "She came from near here and I'm trying to find her people. They said you may know something that might help me."

"Best come and sit then," the old man said and shuffled his way towards a bench at the rear of his hut.

Robert and Rothwynn sat beside Wirt. He seemed to increase in stature as the importance of the occasion impressed itself upon him.

He could see enough to know that this was a well-dressed Norman, probably some knight or nobleman, and the girl was Saxon, wealthy too by the looks of things, the way she was dressed. Maybe there could be something in it for him if he could tell them what they wanted to hear. His hopes were dashed immediately.

"I will know if you are lying to me," Robert informed him. "I already know quite a lot about my mother and her background. So I only want to hear the truth." He had not been a good leader without learning to read his men – and he could certainly read the thoughts of this man.

Wirt squirmed a little and changed his mind about telling this accursed Norman only half truths. He looked as though he could be harsh, as were all Normans, harsh and brutal men who should have stayed in their own country.

Like most Saxons, he despised these invaders and would have preferred to be thrusting a knife into this one rather than sitting here and talking together as though they were friends. So he smiled wryly, showing his one remaining tooth, and said, "Of course sir, indeed I would not lie to you."

"Tell me about the village towards the coast then. It's just a few miles south of here. The one that is abandoned. How long ago did the people disappear from there? Do you know?"

"Sir, it were when I were but a lad. The Vikings came and took many of them away."

"Did any of them survive? Escape?" Robert asked.

The old man shrugged. "Not that I know of for sure," he replied. "Maybe some got into the forest but from what I hear'd they were all took or killed."

"Do you remember any of their names? Her father was the leader of the village I believe."

Wirt's brow wrinkled as he thought long and hard about this question. Finally his memory caught hold of a name. "Kenric?" he pondered. "I think maybe I hear'd of a Kenric?" his voice questioning. "No, that not be right. Kenric were the young 'un. Let me think now."

He was still for a few minutes, muttering to himself, searching his memory. Suddenly, "Wolfstan," his voice loud with pride. He had remembered. "It were Wolfstan. He were the chief. Kenric were his boy."

Wolfstan! So he was right. This was her home. His mother had lived here, spent her childhood here. She'd told him that Wolfstan was her father, Kenric her brother. He sat there and put his head in his hands, willing himself not to cry, not to shame himself in front of these people. He'd found what he had hoped to find for so many years – Aerlene's home.

He felt a hand softly on his back, comforting him. Rothwynn. How grateful he was for her. She understood his longing and his relief. Lifting his face, he looked up at her and managed a smile.

"This is it," he confided softly, his voice filled with emotion. After taking a few minutes to control his feelings, he stood up and turned to shake Wirt's hand. "Thank you Wirt," he said. "I have longed to find this place for many years."

"Your Ma?" Wirt questioned, "She still alive then?"

"No, she died several years ago. But she told me of this place and talked about it with much affection." He handed Wirt a gold coin. "Take this," he offered. "I know it won't buy your freedom but it may help a little." He turned to the man who seemed to be the leader of the villagers. "Is there a market town near here? One that you are free to go to?"

The man nodded and pointed north. "Just a few miles that way," he replied.

"Then please have this," Robert insisted and handed the man a small pouch of money.

"Use it to help these people," he said, indicating the villagers.

"If your Lord finds out about this visit, just tell him that Robert de Sellé came to look for his mother's home. He'll know who I am. But don't tell him about the money," he added with a grin. "He may try to take it from you."

"He be not too bad for a Norman," Wirt muttered as he watched them ride away.

They returned to Aerlene's village and Robert stood and looked around for the largest of the remains. Wolfstan had been the leader of this village, his house would have been the biggest, maybe almost as big as Rothwynn's hall. He hunted through the wreckage of the buildings hoping for some sign for what could have been her home. He was years too late – there was not enough left to show which one was her home.

But he had found her village. He knew where she'd lived and had such a happy childhood. Now he was loth to leave so Rothwynn suggested they stayed overnight. They chose one of the least dilapidated of the old houses to sleep in, their escort found another, then they made things comfortable before they built a fire, had a meal, then sat in the twilight soaking up the atmosphere while Robert reminisced about his mother's childhood.

It was cold so they bundled up together wrapped in blankets, close to the old walls of the house. It gave protection from the wind and fortunately it didn't rain as there was no roof. They could hear the other men chatting late into the night and sounds from the countryside round about, sounds of movement from the local inhabitants, little nocturnal animals out foraging for their dinner or calling for their mates.

Everything seemed so peaceful they finally slept despite the cold but woke early; chilled and ready to wend their way homeward, their provisions getting low and their mission accomplished.

CHAPTER 11

They'd been back home for a week when Rothwynn walked into the compound one morning to find Robert waiting for her.

"Come," he announced. "I have a surprise for you," and he led her to the stables.

There waiting for her was the prettiest mare she'd ever seen. She had been well groomed and her golden brown hair shone, her mane and tail slightly darker. Rothwynn loved her on sight. Her eyes were bright with delight. "For me?" she asked him excitedly.

"Indeed for you," he smiled. "A small token of my love for you, my thanks for your love and understanding. And because you deserve her. I hope she will in some small way make up for your loss of Freya. You like her?"

"Oh Robert, I love her. Thank you so much. How can I ever thank you?"

"I can think of a way," he answered with a smile that made her hide her face in the horse's neck so he couldn't see her blush. Then she turned, stretched up and kissed him on the cheek, and back again to fondle the mare who nuzzled her in return.

"You are such a beautiful creature," she murmured. "I think I'll call you Honey. May I?" she asked turning to Robert.

"Of course, she's yours now. Honey is a perfect name for her. She's the right colour and very sweet." And so Honey she became.

Rothwynn made time every day to ride Honey. Sometimes early in the morning she would ride alone, through the fields nearby, down the lanes and skirting around the forest. At other times she and Robert would go together, further afield, spending a whole afternoon riding north to explore the Cotswold hills or venturing south into the Salisbury plain, wonderful times they treasured.

Rothwynn's days were filled with light now. She loved Robert with all her heart and felt she was beginning to understand him and she knew that he loved her too. He'd opened up all his feelings to her, not just his love for her and his gratitude for the way she filled his life with love and happiness, a happiness that he hadn't felt since he was a young man before his mother had died, but he'd expressed all that Aerlene had meant to him, how he had longed to see her birthplace and get a feel for her childhood, how close he had felt to her and the sadness that enveloped him when she died.

He admitted that he hadn't felt alive again until the day he saw Rothwynn standing at the door of the hall when she'd tried so hard to be brave at a time when her whole world had collapsed. Something about her had pierced the icy armour he'd built around himself, so he was ready to live again. He had known in that minute that he wanted her to be his wife.

It had taken a little longer before he realised he was in love with her, but now he knew he wouldn't want to live without her. She had brought the joy back into his life. He was happier now than he'd ever been, had ever thought possible.

Rothwynn even understood the reason he'd been so harsh in his treatment of her and her people in the beginning, how he'd had to separate himself from his personal feelings and treat them all as the enemy or he could not have coped with the situation.

There had been Robert, the man, the person she loved, and Robert, the army commander who had a village to subdue, a people to rule over. Two distinct peoples with different languages and customs to mould into one. He had begun as the commander and evolved into her Robert, this loving, caring and clever man, whose ideas and hard work seemed, at last, to be having success.

The days were busy. Robert was involved with all the running of the estate and it was a thriving business now – he had made it so. His leadership, control and understanding of everything about the land and the farm amazed Rothwynn. He worked and helped with it all; planning, planting, harvesting, lambing.

He even had an interest in the running of the household, although he never interfered with her decisions or the way she ruled the servants. He also drilled his men in military skills, skills that they must keep sharp in these days of turmoil and trouble on every side.

Rothwynn's days too, were busy with the household. There were the servants to supervise in the kitchens, the dairy, the laundry and the gardens, the feeding of the animals, preparation of the meals and care of the children. Often she could be seen working as hard as anyone; cleaning, cooking, churning – whatever needed doing she was there to help.

She had developed a small herbarium where she made simple medicines from herbs she'd grown and plants that could be harvested from the wild. Rothwynn took good care of the women. If they were sick she treated them and insisted they rested until better.

The Hall was a pleasant place to work – their people knew they were lucky to be there and not with some hard taskmaster. Robert may be a Norman but he had their interests at heart and Rothwynn they had known and loved all her life. They were content.

The evening was the favourite time of Rothwynn's day, once the work was done, the evening meal over, the servants about their work or gone to their homes, and she and Robert were alone.

They would sit on a bench in the hall, by the fire in the cooler weather, and discuss their day and their plans for the next day. Sometimes they would talk, sometimes he would ask her to sing one of his favourite songs to him, or they would read to one another and then he would take her hand and they would go to bed and sleep with his arms holding her close to his heart. The perfect end to the day.

Rothwynn was still not with child. What if she was unable to conceive now? It worried her, especially now that she knew she loved Robert and longed to have his child. What if losing her first baby had damaged her in some way?

It was considered a woman's duty to provide an heir for her husband. She would be thought of as a failure if she was barren. Robert needed a son but he didn't criticise her at all and she loved him all the more for it.

He was always so considerate of her now, deferring to her wishes and listening if she ever had advice to offer him. He'd realised early on that she knew her people well and she knew a lot about the running of the compound and the farming of their land, and consequently left her in complete charge of the running of the household.

So when she suggested that they ask Father Bernard to once again bless their marriage bed, he readily agreed.

After the blessing, they redoubled their efforts and Rothwynn was with child at last…her baby due sometime early next summer.

Christmas arrived again and they had much to celebrate. Although many had died during the attack by Aelfric, they had made it through. The harvest had been bountiful, several babies had been born, and only one woman died during childbirth.

Rothwynn's maid, Willa, and Raoul had a son, and even Annis, who'd been married to Robert's steward, was expecting another child.

Rothwynn had not been surprised when Annis had approached her and told her that she and Louis wanted to be married. She'd watched with interest as the romance blossomed.

Of all Robert's men Louis was Rothwynn's favourite. She had worked with him in the running of the household since their arrival and had come to know him well. He was quiet, kind and well spoken. She always thought of him as a gentle man and learned that he'd been married but his wife had died several years before – they'd had no children.

Rothwynn knew he admired Annis and even encouraged him to approach her, talk to her, get to know her as Annis too, was lonely. She had her little daughter, who brought her a great deal of joy, but she needed companionship as well. Rothwynn was delighted to know that it seemed to be working well… that they wanted to wed. She noticed how Annis' eyes lit up when Louis entered the room, the way they smiled at each other, the quiet conversations.

It had begun when Louis, last winter, covered in snow, walked into the Hall. He stood in the doorway stamping his feet, brushing his fingers through his hair and shaking his cloak free of the snow. At first the darkness of the Hall obscured his vision of the large room.

It wasn't until his eyes had adjusted from the brightness outside that he noticed her, Annis, in the opposite corner of the room, sitting with her baby daughter talking softly to the child. He stood transfixed. Annis looked so beautiful as she gazed lovingly at her little girl, smiling at her and caressing the tiny cheeks. Hardly daring to breathe, he hesitantly approached her.

He wanted her so much to be his wife. He loved her with a depth he hadn't believed he could ever feel again. If only she could love him too. Annis heard him walk towards her and looked up at him. The smile she gave him made his heart begin to pound.

"Oh, Annis," he implored as he reached her side. "I do love you so very much. I want to take care of you and the child. I want you for my wife. Could you love me enough to marry me? To spend the rest of your life with me?"

Annis was silent for a moment or two and Louis thought she was going to refuse him. Then she spoke and her voice was soft and at once he knew it was going to be all right. "Of course I will marry you. I love you too," she responded and her smile was radiant.

"I was happy enough with Selwyn," Annis explained to Rothwynn later. "I liked him and was sorry when he died but I didn't love him. I really love Louis. I feel alive and happy when I'm with him. And he says he feels the same about me."

"I am immensely pleased for you," Rothwynn reassured her. "Louis is a wonderful man. I like him very much and hope you will have a wonderful life together."

They'd been married for several months now and were both excited about the coming child.

CHAPTER 12

On the tenth day of June Rothwynn's son was born. Her labour lasted over thirty-six hours and she could not believe the intensity of the pain. It felt as though she was being torn in half over and over again.

Robert had listened to her moans and cries but when he tried to enter her chamber the women turned him away. "It's not fitting," he was told. He suffered it for almost a day and then forced his way into the room to be by her side.

The room was hot and dark and to Robert it seemed as though it was filled with every woman who lived or worked in the Hall. Rothwynn was standing behind a chair, leaning over and moaning softly as another contraction made its presence felt. She was dressed only in her shift and it clung to her, damp with sweat. He walked to her and she grabbed his hand.

"Don't go, don't leave me. Please don't leave me," she begged him, her voice sounding weak.

"I'm not going anywhere. I'll stay with you until our child is born."

He walked over to the window and threw the shutters open. There was an immediate outcry. "They need to be shut. We must keep her safe from the outside air," he was told. Ignoring them, he turned and asked Willa, "Do all these women need to be here?"

Willa shook her head.

"What are they doing here then?"

"They are here to give support and because they love her."

"Yes, well I will give her all the love and support that she needs. Where is Werberga? She's the midwife, isn't she?"

"I'm here sir," Werberga replied, her voice coming from the other side of the room where she appeared to be busy arranging baby clothes.

"Everyone else, out!" Robert demanded in his authoritative voice. "Willa, Rothwynn will need you, please stay." He ushered the women out then turned again to Willa. "Please fetch me a bowl of tepid water and several clean, dry cloths," he asked, then returned to Rothwynn and helped her back to the bed where he sat her down.

"Robert, help me. I can't do this. I can't take any more." She could barely speak, her voice hoarse.

"Yes you can. You're my brave, strong girl. You can do it," he reassured her. "I'll be here with you. I'll not leave you, I promise."

When Willa returned with the water and cloths, he removed Rothwynn's clothing and gently washed her body then dried her and dressed her in a clean shift. By now the heat in the room was lessening and Rothwynn seemed calmer and finding it easier to breathe.

Robert stayed by her side talking softly to her and encouraging her, wiping her face and her hands, and holding her tenderly in his arms as she strained to bring their child into the world. Finally, when she was completely exhausted, it was over and their long-awaited baby boy arrived. Still he held her in his arms comforting and caressing her while Werberga did what was necessary for both mother and child.

"I told you you could do it," Robert said, his voice filled with emotion and love for his wife. "I'm so proud of you little mother. I adore you."

"The baby?" she queried.

"A boy, and he's perfect," he responded, "You've given me my son and if I live to be a hundred I can never thank you enough or express how much I love you."

Only when she was comfortable, at ease, did he hold his son. Then he took their baby to Rothwynn and as she held him to her breast Robert sat beside her and silently thanked God for this great blessing in his life. Not just a wife he adored, but now he had his son as well.

They called him William, in honour of the King. Rothwynn had argued vehemently against it. She had wanted him named for her father.

"You know I would do almost anything for you but I cannot do this. He is a Norman child, and for better or worse, this is now a Norman country," Robert told her. "He cannot be known by a Saxon name. You don't understand my love," he added. "It will be easier for him during his life if he has a Norman name. Saxon names will not be popular with the rulers of this country in the years ahead. I want what is best for him."

Rothwynn understood what he was telling her but she despised the Norman King. Robert, in almost every way, would defer to his wife, but in this he would not be moved. The baby was baptised by Father Bernard in their new church, William de Sellé.

CHAPTER 13

It had been another good spring. The ploughing and planting had gone well. Their livestock was increasing and things were calm and peaceful. There'd been no more trouble with vagrants or outlaws either. Robert kept firm control over his demesne and guarded his possessions with vigilance. He'd learned his lesson well. Now that he had his son there was all the more reason for him to secure a good inheritance to leave for his descendants.

Unfortunately, elsewhere in the country things were not going as well. Disturbances were flaring up everywhere and the King demanded help from those he'd entrusted with land. All able bodied men were to report to him in London with as many men as they could muster. Robert had to leave to serve and fight for the King.

Rothwynn knew that more Saxons would be killed in the uprisings. They would be taught who was master here. These Normans were ruthless in clamping down on any disturbances. William would have peace in his realm no matter how many Saxons, or Normans, died in the attempt.

Her fear was for Robert, for herself if he should be killed in the fighting, and for their son if anything should happen to his father. Rothwynn's heart ached for her country but it ached more for her own little portion of England. For now they had peace, but would it stay that way if Robert wasn't there to take control?

The night before they were due to leave Rothwynn repeated her fears to Robert.

"Promise me you will come back to me and to William," she begged him.

"You know I will," he assured her, "These uprisings don't last long, and do not usually cause much damage to our soldiers. We are well trained and most of the Saxons are not. It may even be over before we get there and I will be home before you know I've gone." He tried to comfort her and convince himself that it would be so.

Robert left her in charge with a small group of men to guard the compound and Father Bernard blessed the company before they left. Robert kissed her and young William goodbye, mounted his horse, gave the order, and they were gone. Rothwynn knew they'd be back before winter, maybe even before the harvest, if the men were gone for too long the whole country would starve. But who would come back? Some of them may never return.

Her whole body was filled with fear as they rode away. This time she climbed the hill behind the hall and watched as they departed, the sight of them getting smaller and smaller as they disappeared into the distance. She watched until they were completely out of sight, her heart heavy, almost in despair.

Her despair was not only for Robert and his men, many of whom she had come to know and like, but also for the Saxons, men, women and children who had been dispossessed of their homes and land. Their formerly peaceful lives gone forever.

Now they faced another threat, another fight for their freedom, simply because they had dared to rebel against this invasion of their country. How she hated the Bastard conqueror.

Robert and his company of soldiers had been gone for ten days when the first theft occurred. Not much, just a little food and no one was hurt. Three days later two hens disappeared. Neither time did anyone see any strangers in the area or signs of a break-in. She discussed it with Father Bernard.

"We must double the guard," he insisted. "But we have so few men to spare. They'll need to take shifts through the night, seeing as though that's when the thefts are taking place, and after working all day in the fields it's a lot to expect of them to stay awake all night, too."

"Then the women will take turns working in the fields," Rothwynn decided. "They're used to helping with the harvest. They'll know what to do."

So it was arranged that the women would take over the bulk of the farm work. They already did quite a lot of it anyway, but it would put an extra burden on them as they would still be required to work in the kitchen and dairy, to do the milking and feeding of the animals, and to take care of the children and the household.

Half expecting some grumbles from the women at the extra workload required of them, Rothwynn was relieved that her suggestion was accepted with resignation and approval. The men would form a round-the-clock guard and they would take time each day to hone their fighting skills. Rothwynn knew that Robert would approve of the plan.

It was a busy time for them all. Rothwynn fell into bed at night exhausted. Little William took up much of her time and she did her share of the work with the other women, several of them having babies too. Others were heavy with child.

They divided up the workload and toiled tirelessly side by side, but it was successful. The outlaws must have been aware that they were better guarded because no more incursions occurred. If they had a leader, he was definitely not another Aelfric. The women even managed the harvest with limited help from the men.

Rothwynn had hoped that Robert would be back by the time the harvest was brought in. It had been such hard and heavy work. Each day she hoped to hear that Robert was coming home, each night she missed him more and more. But they'd had no news for weeks. It was well into October before they heard that Robert and his men were on their way home.

Once more Rothwynn climbed the hill every day watching the horizon to the southeast for signs of them coming, but this time she was longing for a glimpse of them, this time she was longing for them to arrive. She smiled to herself as she remembered how she had felt that first time and how she had dreaded their arrival.

After a week of looking, she climbed the hill once more, Annis and Willa beside her. All three of them nervously scanning the horizon to the south east. "I see them," Willa excitedly exclaimed. Running down the hill and into the compound, "They're home," Rothwynn called to everyone. "They're almost here."

Everyone ran out to welcome the men, but the silent questions hung in the air. Would they all be there? Who would be missing or injured? The thought made them extremely nervous as so many men are wounded or killed in battle. Several of them had become fathers while they were gone. Would the new children have a father?

They entered the compound. Rothwynn searched for sight of Robert and almost sobbed with relief when she saw him. As he dismounted from his horse, she ran straight into his arms, tears streaming down her face.

They clung to each other for several minutes before she pulled away from him, "You've been injured," she exclaimed, concern immediately showing on her face. "Your arm is hurt."

"It's nothing," he reassured her. "A sword cut, but it's healing well."

It took him a few minutes to convince her he was fine before she said, "You need to see William. He's grown so much."

Arm in arm they walked into the Hall so he could greet his son. He'd been less than two weeks old when Robert last saw him.

Miraculously all Robert's men were alive but several of them had serious injuries. Some, like Robert, minor cuts and bruises. They feasted that evening and once again Robert pulled her to her feet before the end.

"Come," he smiled. "It's time for us to retire."

But this time she needed no encouragement to follow him.

CHAPTER 14

There was great cause to be celebrating at Christmas; a successful harvest, their men home safely, the peace they enjoyed in their little corner of the world, and Rothwynn was with child again. They made the most of the twelve days of feasting.

But the New Year brought miserable weather. It was so cold that everything froze, even the water in the buckets inside the buildings were thickly covered with ice each morning. On warmer days the ground would thaw and turn into deep ruts of mud and then freeze again, causing a couple of the horses to fall and break their legs and then had to be destroyed.

A few of the children became gravely ill with a coughing sickness and died, along with several of the old folk. It was a sad time for them all.

Rothwynn grieved for the families who had lost their loved ones and gave what help and support that was needed. She constantly worried about William, but he remained healthy and thrived.

Fortunately spring came early and was warm and beautiful. The ploughing and planting was done in record time and before long it was June and William's first birthday. He was already trying to walk, taking several steps at a time, and making his wants and needs understood. And then it was August and Rothwynn's second child was due.

The women tried to keep Robert out of her chamber but they did not succeed. He demanded to be there from the beginning and once more insisted that only Werberga and Willa were present and the window wide open. Whether it was because he was there, or because it was her second baby, it was easier for her this time.

Another healthy boy. Robert was elated. "We'll call him Gilbert, after my father," he announced.

Rothynn knew it was pointless to ask that he be called for her father. Robert would always insist on Norman names for his children and she understood why he wanted it that way, but although she tried to accept his decision, it was always there, in the back of her mind. So he was baptised Gilbert and grew as strong and healthy as his brother.

The seasons came and went; ploughing, planting, and harvesting. Sometimes Robert had to leave when the King demanded his loyal followers to defend some part of the country from Saxon uprisings, but always he came home with most, if not all, of his men. Their community thrived and was peaceful.

When Gilbert was two years old, Rothwynn had her first daughter, named Mathilda for the King's wife. Robert was just as thrilled with his daughter as he'd been with his sons, and as Mathilda got older she enchanted her father and could get him to do almost anything her heart desired.

There were times in her life when Rothwynn couldn't believe how lucky she'd been with her husband. She recalled the day he'd arrived, taking over her home and forcing her to marry him, and of the first days of their marriage and how he'd treated in bed, and allowed his men to take the other Saxon women.

She remembered how she had hated him then... him and his Bastard King, although she still hated the King. Sometimes Robert would be summoned to appear before him and he would ask her if she'd like to go with him.

"No, thank you. I prefer not to meet the man who destroyed my country," she would reply. "I hope he rots in hell for what he's done."

She had absolutely no qualms telling him how she felt now. Robert would only smile.

"Just don't go looking at any of the other women," she warned.

"Never fear," he reassured her. "I've got all the woman I want right here. And I'll be back as quickly as

I can. I'd rather not go at all. I'd much rather be here, at home with you and the children."

And she knew he meant it.

Sometimes, when he returned from these visits to the King, Rothwynn would ask him to tell her about the places and people he'd seen, as though she was trying to picture everything in her mind. She wanted to know about the Queen, the court, the buildings, what was happening to people in different parts of her country.

He knew she ached for the sufferings of her people, the Saxons. She was happy to know that the Pope had ordered William pay penance for the number of people killed during the Battle of Hastings and its aftermath, but her response had been, "Too little, too late."

She realised that it really wouldn't make any difference to the way William treated the Saxons still living. The King had decided to build an Abbey on the battle site. The high altar would be where Harold was thought to have been killed. So far the building, and the penance, were only in the planning stages. Robert sometimes wondered to himself if it would ever be completed.

Rothwynn was with child again, although this time she was ill. Not just morning sickness, she was used to that, but with pains she hadn't experienced before. The days seemed to drag on with her body aching and her hands and feet swelling. She tried to rest but with three children to care for and the household to run, it proved difficult.

She and Robert found some time to be alone and they cherished the moments they spent together. He was exceedingly gentle with her and treated her with tenderness all the time. Her love for him was now so deep, she could not imagine her life without him by her side.

When the time came for her child to be born, once again Robert insisted on being with her and she was grateful for his presence. It gave her courage with him there, to know he cared enough for her to want to take part in this important occasion for their family.

At first the other men had laughed at him for his concern and his obvious devotion to his wife, but it didn't last. They had deep respect for him as their leader, his discipline always being firm but fair, so his unusual behaviour was accepted as somewhat eccentric and then ignored.

Their fourth child was a girl, and the birth was relatively easy, but when her pains continued, Warberga realised there was another child coming. Twins. That explained the difficult time she'd had for the past months. A second girl was born. Robert named them Aline and Adela after his sisters. Rothwynn never completely regained her previous robust health, but soon she was up and going about her duties, caring for her family and overseeing the other women.

She adored her two baby girls as much as she did her three older children and realised that she was extremely blessed. Five beautiful, healthy children and a husband who obviously loved her deeply and showed his love and concern for his family every day. With a large family to care for now, the times that she and Robert spent together were even more precious than before and were treasured by them both.

As their children grew older, they took lessons from Father Bernard, Rothwynn taught them when they were very young. She'd been taught to read and write, as it had been encouraged among her people since the time of the great Saxon King, Alfred, and she wanted all her children to follow this Saxon tradition. The Normans sometimes educated their boys born to noble families, but never the girls.

Robert was a little amazed at her decision, but as his children seemed quite content learning to read and write and as he had always allowed Rothwynn to run the household as she wished, he did little more than raise his eyebrows occasionally and became more and more proud of their accomplishments as they got older.

Robert and Rothwynn cherished the times they spent together and with their children. Occasionally they'd go for long walks through the forest, or have picnics on the hillside.

Robert taught their children to ride almost as soon as they could walk as his father had done with him, and they'd go for long rides through the beautiful countryside that would last for hours. Sometimes the two of them would sit and watch the children playing together, his arm around her or holding hands like young lovers, and he would whisper to her, telling her how much he loved her and how precious she was.

Robert occasionally took William and Gilbert to visit friends where they could practise their fighting skills with boys their own age, a necessary exercise in this time of constant threat. During those days Rothwynn would worry as it was not uncommon for young boys to be seriously hurt while learning these much needed skills, but her fears were unfounded. Always they came home again, whole and healthy and bursting with energy, confident in their growing abilities.

At home there were plenty of children to play with. Both Annis and Willa had several young ones, the boys all played together, pretending to be knights and having sword fights with little wooden swords that Robert made for them. The girls too, were friends, and sometimes watched the boys and cheered them on, giggling to each other and poking gentle fun at their brothers.

There were evenings when, before the children went to bed, they would have music time in the hall, with Rothwynn teaching them the songs and ballads she'd learned as a child. Before long they would all join in and Mathilda became quite a gifted musician, playing the lyre while her brothers played the flute and drum, bringing back memories of times when Rothwynn had played with her brothers. Robert would sit and watch his family, overflowing with love for them all.

Family play times were Rothwynn's favourite times of all. Robert was always so busy that the few hours each week that they could spend together were treasured. It was usually in the evening. The winter evenings they would gather around the fire in the Hall and he would take one of the children on to his knee and tell stories of his childhood, or she would recite ancient Saxon sagas to them. The younger ones enjoyed rides on Robert's back as he pretended to be the horse and ride around the room or chase them, pretending to be a hungry wolf, and delighted screams would follow.

The long summer twilight they usually enjoyed outside. The boys' favourite was when they would try to hit a ball thrown by their father and run away before it could be caught or thrown back. The girls enjoyed him carrying them around on his shoulders and seeing how tall they could be.

Even times when they worked together were made into some sort of game. They all loved going to the orchard and picking fruit, especially if it was high in the trees and Robert had to hold them up to reach or the boys tried climbing as high as possible. Whatever they did was fun and it was together, and always very memorable.

There were feast days that were special, too. The first celebrated each year was May Day, the return of the sun. The morning was busy with the preparations then they had a great feast in the Hall.

Later everyone would gather outside where, by tradition, the boys had cut a large branch from a tree, the longest and straightest they could find, and stuck it in the ground. Then all the girls put flowers in their hair and danced around the tree while a huge bonfire burned in the compound for all to enjoy.

Midsummer was enjoyed by everyone, celebrating the power of the sun over darkness. Once more there was feasting and a bonfire, the children often dressed up and had a parade. Robert and Rothwynn began a tradition of their own. They watched the sunrise from the hill outside the compound, sitting in the grove of trees, and discovered that if there had indeed been an altar there in days long past, the sun's rays would have hit the centre of it when they first appeared over the horizon.

Harvest time was another great cause for celebration. At Michaelmas there was reason for rejoicing with the harvest safely gathered in, providing for the long, dark, winter months. The last sheaf of wheat from the harvest was formed into a corn dolly, woven into a human shape and given the place of honour on the harvest feast table. The corn dolly represented Mother Earth and was believed to bring good fortune and good crops in the coming season.

But Christmas was the favourite time of year for them all. They'd have a family outing to the forest to find the evergreens they needed for decorating the Hall, large bunches of holly and ivy, then spend hours deciding where to put it all.

Finding an old tree branch large enough to use as the Yule log was another enjoyable task. The boys would run through the trees shouting to each other, "How about this one," or "I think I've found one," and then finally drag one home.

Candles too, were used on the table turning the Hall into a fairyland for the girls to enjoy. The music and dancing and feasting were traditions enjoyed by everyone.

Perhaps the favourite was the Saxon tradition of the Wassail bowl when the huge cup was passed from hand to hand and everyone drank from it. Robert would shout to one and all "Be well," and they would shout back, "Drink and be healthy."

But Rothwynn and Robert didn't allow the children to miss the special significance of these holy days, making sure they understood the importance of the birth of the Christ Child and the visits of the angels to the shepherds and the wise men arriving with gifts, following the new star in the heavens.

Rothwynn filled their home with love and joy. The Hall was always ringing with the sound of happy children, their own and the other children who lived in the compound.

Animals too. Rothwynn often seemed to have little orphaned lambs, just hatched chicks or a young wild animal that had been hurt in some way that she was caring for. Pet dogs and cats were always around, patiently putting up with the children playing with them, the girls often treating puppies or kittens as toys and their laughter filled Robert with happiness.

There were times when Rothwynn wondered how long life like this could go on. It seemed to her that it was almost too perfect.

CHAPTER 15

When the twins were almost five years old Rothwynn discovered she was with child again. She'd actually hoped not to be, although she knew Robert would be thrilled to have another son. Not that he preferred his sons to his daughters. If anything it was the other way round, but he desired to establish a dynasty and he needed male heirs, so she accepted it with resignation and hoped her health would be better this time, and it was for the first few weeks.

But as the months went by she felt herself becoming weaker. Sometimes she was in tears for no apparent reason. Sometimes she had difficulty breathing and she had to rest. She was uneasy… wondering if something was wrong. No, not just wondering, knowing that something was wrong.

Not wanting to worry Robert, and hoping that she was imagining it all, she spoke to Werberga. The midwife's advice was to rest more and she prepared a potion of herbs for her to drink each day, which did seem to help and eased her fears for a short while. But soon the worry came back.

Robert was even more solicitous than before, although she tried not to worry him. The baby was a boy, born too early and was extremely weak. It was obvious he would not survive, but Werberga didn't tell her, as she knew that Rothwynn was dying too, and so did Robert. With his heart breaking he turned away so she couldn't see him crying.

"Robert," she whispered.

Wiping away his tears, he turned back to her immediately. "Yes my love?" his voice full of love and concern.

"No, I mean I want him called Robert. Please?"

"As you wish," he said, now his voice was husky with the tears he couldn't stop as he watched helplessly as Rothwynn slipped slowly away.

He called Father Bernard. Using the holy water, the priest made the sign of the cross on the baby's head and named him Robert. They gave the child to his mother but she was so weak she could scarcely hold him, so Robert held them both tenderly in his arms wanting to hold her close to him forever.

Her breathing became shallower and she turned and smiled at him. "I love you so much," she told him, her voice so soft he could barely hear her. "You have made me so happy." Then Rothwynn took one last deep breath, shuddered and was still.

As though the child knew his mother was dead, he whimpered and then his breathing stopped.

Lying them both gently on the bed, Robert bent forward and kissed his beloved wife, Rothwynn; first her hands, then her breast, her cheeks, her forehead and her mouth. "Goodbye my love," he whispered, tears streaming down his face. He reached his finger out to caress his little son then buried his face in his hands and sobbed.

Mother and son were buried together, next to the altar in their little church. Robert left instructions that when the time came, he was to be buried with them.

Father Bernard gave him a letter that Rothwynn had written.

Robert, my love,
I know that I am dying. This time I will not survive the birth of our baby. I am not afraid to die, but oh how I will miss you, the sound of your voice, the feel of your arms around me, to see you with our children. I hate that bastard who invaded and raped my country but I cannot be sorry that he came because he brought you to me. You have filled my body with our children, my heart with love and my life with joy. I will be so lonely without you, but for now you have to stay behind to care for our home and our land, to make safe the inheritance for our children. I will be waiting for you when it is time for you to join me. And then my soul will delight in you for eternity.
Forever, your loving wife,
Rothwynn.

CHAPTER 16

For weeks Robert went around in a daze. Everything he did was done without thinking, through habit. The only time he felt any joy was with his children – they needed him more now that their mother was gone, so they grieved together.

The only place that he found any peace and comfort was on the hill. He spent hours there, sitting by the grove of trees and feeling her presence. She had loved this place so much and he felt as though her spirit was still there, but his arms were empty without her and he ached for her.

But life went on and after a few months Robert took on another project. He decided to build an Abbey and dedicate it to the memory of his wife. He didn't neglect his other duties, his land or his children, but he spent a vast amount of time, money and energy on the Abbey. He needed it to be perfect…for her.

It took a couple of years before it was finished, and upon completion he asked Father Bernard to be in charge, at least for the time being.

The good priest turned him down. "I'm too old now," he affirmed. "Maybe twenty years ago I would have accepted your offer, but not now."

Instead Robert sent for his younger brother Armand who'd entered the church, and he arrived with the blessing of an order of Benedictines in Normandy. They would be aligned with the monastery there.

As the years went by the community continued to thrive. Robert retained excellent control over his people, still spent time overseeing the running of his demesne and time with his children.

But he spent more and more time at the Abbey; time in reflection, meditation and prayer. He desperately missed Rothwynn. He'd never replaced her – never even looked at another woman, and he knew he never would. She'd been his love and his life while she was on the earth, and she would be his again in Heaven. He knew deep down in his heart and soul that it was so, but he yearned for her physical presence beside him, even though he knew her spiritual presence was always there.

Occasionally he'd have conversations with her, asking her advice about this or that or someone, and her answers would come into his mind. And as he grew older he felt her closeness more and more. He no longer had to visit the hill to feel her beside him, although he still visited the grove of trees whenever he felt the need, but it seemed she was always close to him, comforting and cherishing him, listening to his very thoughts. If it wasn't for his children he would have wished he could join her sooner rather than later, but they still needed him.

William was growing into a fine young man. Rothwynn would've been so proud of her eldest son. He hoped that somehow she could see him and know how well he was doing. Gilbert too, was progressing nicely – a choice young man, good at arms, and popular with his peers.

But there was no doubt that Robert was entranced with his daughters. They all, in one way or another, reminded him of Rothwynn, bringing her presence into their home. He dreaded the time when they would leave his care and be married, but for now he made the most of having them with him. They were a great comfort to him.

William and the twin girls were fair, with dark blue eyes like their mother, although their hair was a shade or two darker than hers had been. Both Gilbert and Mathilda had brown hair and eyes like their father.

But Mathilda was the one that reminded him most of Rothwynn. She had her mother's love of music, the love of her country and her home. Sometimes he would hear her voice and for just a split second would think that it was Rothwynn. In the evenings Mathilda would sit close to him, take his hand in hers and talk to him softly about her mother. He treasured those special times with his eldest daughter.

Aline and Adela had Rothwynn's smile and cheery disposition, the same determined chin and sprinkle of freckles across their noses. Sometimes, if he caught an unexpected glimpse of either of them, he would for one brief moment imagine it was Rothwynn home again, which brought the pain of losing her once more.

Thankfully, as time went on, the feelings lessened and he appreciated the reminders of his beloved wife.

William was the one who took it upon himself to care for Honey, Rothwynn's much loved horse. He would groom her and ride her every day.

Once Robert came upon William in the stables. He'd been for a ride and just returned, had been brushing the horse when overcome with sadness and buried his head in Honey's neck and sobbed. Robert put his arms around his son and they cried together.

William had also inherited his mother's love of learning and enjoyed reading. He loved music but hadn't the talent for playing or singing that Rothwynn had, but would love to hear his sisters when they had musical evenings, although he was quite adept at playing the drums and would occasionally accompany the girls.

Robert had often wondered if Gilbert had been Rothwynn's favourite child. He'd never noticed any favouritism but sometimes he would catch her looking at their second son. She'd have a dreamy look in her eyes and a half smile on her lips, as though she was reminded of something special.

Maybe it was because of all their children, Gilbert was the one most like him. The older he grew the more like his father he became. He remembered once coming upon Rothwynn watching the children play. Her eyes were upon Gilbert and as she heard Robert enter the Hall, she'd turned and smiled at him.

"I think that Gilbert must look just as you did at the same age. I wish I could ask your mother if she'd agree."

Gilbert was the one who would have to make his own way in the world, and he had the determination and skill to do it. He had Rothwynn's sunny disposition but also her courage. He kept his feelings under control and rarely showed emotion.

Only once did Robert find Gilbert weeping for the loss of his mother and it almost broke his heart to see his son so inconsolable. He'd wept for his son, for all his children losing their mother. He remembered with a deep sadness the loss he'd felt when his own mother had died. He too had been inconsolable.

Occasionally there were evenings when they would gather together around the fire in the Hall and the children would ask him questions about Rothwynn. What was her childhood like? Why had she married him when she hated Normans so much? What was her family like? On and on the questions went.

He would answer them all as frankly as possible and sometimes they would sit late into the night just talking about her. He wanted his children to know all about their mother and to appreciate and never forget their heritage or how brave she'd been in facing such difficult times alone.

He tried to paint a verbal picture of how she'd looked as she stood in the doorway of the Hall to face the invaders, not knowing what was going to happen to her or her people, knowing that her family had all been killed by the Normans.

He told them of her courage, her spirit as she condemned the king, not caring how Robert felt about her opinion. He thought she'd even have told the king himself if she'd had the opportunity. He'd been thoroughly enchanted with her.

He told them how beautiful she was and how they'd come to love each other so very much, how proud she had been of them all and how she would love to see them…be with them now. Then he would add, "I think she can. I think she watches over all of us. There are times when I can feel her here, almost hear her voice. She will never leave us."

And they would sit quietly contemplating and feeling her closeness.

Eventually a wife was found for William. He was now seventeen and old enough to be betrothed. Her name was Maud and she was twelve. They would be married when she was fifteen but until then she would live with them and become accustomed to their ways and the home that one day she would control. She was a quiet, shy child but made friends with Mathilda and soon was giggling and playing with her future sisters and fitting easily into their lives.

Robert realised that it would soon be Mathilda's turn to leave home and marry. He was determined to find a good husband for her, one that would treat her well. And then Aline and Adela would go.

His heart was heavy. How he longed for Rothwynn. He so wanted to be able to discuss it with her. She'd told him how she'd been so frightened of Aelfric when her father betrothed her to him and Robert didn't want that for his daughters, so he spent time visiting old friends and meeting their sons before making any decisions.

When the time finally came for Mathilda to leave, he felt she was tearing his heart out. He'd done his best for her and chosen a young man that he felt Rothwynn would approve of, a son of a leading family, wealthy enough to provide well for her and who treated his people fairly. Robert thought he'd be kind to his precious daughter.

Gilbert joined himself to a leading family too, as a soldier, and set off to make his fortune, just as his father had done years before.

William and Maud were married and within a year had a child, a boy they named Robert. He was touched that they named the child for him. His dynasty had begun… His dream fulfilled.

Within five years his two younger daughters, Aline and Adele, had also gone. Married, he hoped, to kind and good husbands. Now he was alone. William had taken over the running of the demesne and was doing an excellent job, leaving Robert free to do as he pleased.

He gave up the secular life and joined the monks in his Abbey, determined to devote the remainder of his life to prayer and good works. He hoped it wouldn't be too long. He still longed for Rothwynn, although he found that there was still much joy in his life.

He was happy in the Abbey and whenever possible his children came to visit him, bringing their children as their families grew. He knew that Rothwynn would have loved being a grandmother and would have doted on her grandchildren…if only…but regrets didn't help.

He concentrated on the positive things in his life: his life at the Abbey, watching William taking exceptional care of Rothwynn's home and his inheritance, his children happy in their marriages and now with families of their own, and frequent visits to the grove of trees on the hill where he communicated with Rothwynn, still feeling her ever closer to him.

As time went on he often wondered what Rothwynn would think of the things that were happening to her country now. He could almost hear the scathing remarks that she would no doubt make about the King's Doomsday book, as it came to be called. "How dare he! Just who does he think he is? This country got on very well without him and his ideas, taxing everyone to fill his coffers. The insolence and greed of the man!"

Perhaps her language would not be quite so tame either. She had never hesitated in calling the king "that Bastard," as all his enemies were wont to do.

And what would she make of the huge castle now being built in London? A massive fort located by the River Thames, with four huge towers, one at each corner and enclosed with mighty walls, built with stone imported from Caen in Normandy. It was meant to subdue the residents of the old Roman city, to impress upon their minds, as if they didn't need reminding, that these Normans were in charge and here to stay.

Another thing he knew would have infuriated her was the formation of forests, or hunting grounds as they were designated. Vast tracts of land where hunting was now forbidden except for the Norman elite. Places where the Saxons, and their predecessors, had hunted for food for thousands of years, now banned under threat of maiming or death.

No doubt this would cause even more suffering for the native people – starvation or outlawry. He couldn't help smiling to himself as he imagined her reaction. Yes, there was no doubt she would've been furious at the way her country was being subjugated. His mother too, would have been equally appalled.

He thought he agreed with her...with them both. Perhaps his Saxon blood was more dominant that he realised.

Each year the Abbey grew. They developed more land, tilled the ground, planted more crops and kept more animals, mainly sheep for their wool. They expanded the buildings and soon it was a thriving enterprise, prospering well from the sale of wool.

Robert was involved with overseeing the repairs to a few of the buildings when necessary, until one day, as he was inspecting storm damage to the roof of the Abbey, he fell. No longer young, with bones broken and internal injuries, he knew he was dying. His children came – all of them. And one by one they sat with him and said their goodbyes. His brother gave him last rites and they knew he was slipping away. With tears in their eyes they stood around his bed.

He opened his eyes and saw them all, smiled and told them he loved them and was proud of them. Then he spoke softly. "Rothwynn," they heard him say, wonder in his voice. "You've come. Is it time then?"

She spoke, but only he could hear the words. "Your work is done here. I want you with me now. I've already waited too long. Come my love," she smiled and held out her hand to him.

They heard his last words. "Oh, my dearest love, how I have longed for you."

He took her hand and they turned to leave. Rothwynn hesitated and looked longingly at her children, as though she would stay a while and embrace them all. "You did well with them I think. Thank you," she whispered to him before they left together.

Young again and hand in hand they wove their way towards Rothwynn's hill, her special place. Hands still clasped they climbed to the summit then stopped and looked back, one last time, at their earthly home. He took her in his arms and kissed her tenderly before they disappeared into the mist.

Together at last... together forever.

THE END OF THE BEGINNING

COMING SOON

ROTHWYNN'S LEGACY is the continuing story of the de Sellé family through the centuries, from the days of Magna Carta, the Black Death, the Wars of the Roses, Civil War and on to the 20th century, following the life and loves of eleven couples affected my major historical events.

For more information on Mary Francis and her books, follow her on Facebook:

https://www.facebook.com/maryfrancisnovels

Printed in Great Britain
by Amazon